D0373341

THE MAN WITH EIGHT PAIRS OF LEGS

Leslie
Kirk
Campbell

SARABANDE BOOKS *Louisville, KY*

THE MAN WITH EIGHT PAIRS OF LEGS

STORIES

Copyright © 2022 by Leslie Kirk Campbell
All rights reserved.

No part of this book may be reproduced without
written permission of the publisher.

Publisher's Cataloging-In-Publication Data
(Prepared by The Donohue Group, Inc.)

Names: Campbell, Leslie Kirk, author.
Title: The man with eight pairs of legs: stories / Leslie Kirk Campbell.
Description: Louisville, KY: Sarabande Books, 2022
Identifiers: ISBN 9781946448880 (paperback)
ISBN 9781946448897 (e-book)
Subjects: LCSH: Risk-taking (Psychology)—Fiction.
Episodic memory—Fiction. | LCGFT: Short stories.
Classification: LCC PS3603.A47729 M36 2022 (print)
LCC PS3603.A47729 (e-book)
DDC 813/.6—dc23

Cover design by Danika Isdahl.
Interior design by Alban Fischer.
Printed in Canada.
This book is printed on acid-free paper.
Sarabande Books is a nonprofit literary organization.

This project is supported in part by an award from the National Endowment
for the Arts. The Kentucky Arts Council, the state arts agency,
supports Sarabande Books with state tax dollars and federal
funding from the National Endowment for the Arts.

For Caryl Joy and Burnham Orlando

CONTENTS

I stand in awe of my body, this matter to which I am
bound has become so strange to me.

HENRY DAVID THOREAU,
The Maine Woods, 1864

INTRODUCTION

Smack in the middle of our chic contemporary postmodern fog, Leslie Kirk Campbell commits the greatest sin possible: she refuses to place intellect over emotion. In doing so she seeks depth instead of dazzle, sentiment in place of cynicism. Without sacrificing the intelligence and writerly skills it takes to do justice to her compelling material, time and again Campbell leads us out of the murk of mere "innovation"—the fetish of the "new"—and into the light of true feeling. As a result, these stories owned me, body and soul. *This* is the sort of fiction I look for to take me into the long night.

I read *The Man with Eight Pairs of Legs* anonymously. I had no biographical details. Despite this, as I read, it became clear to me that the author was a woman, one with a mature voice and vision. There is an admirable authorial patience, allowing her stories as well as her characters to layer, or unfold—depending on the need of each story. This gives the work the complexities of actual human beings, caught as we all are in temperament and time. In fact, time itself could be a character in these stories, as the past (or the life unlived, or an impossible future) stalks her people just as such ghosts stalk us, out here in the "nonfictional" world.

Campbell's people feel genuine throughout this debut collection. Their situations (even when fraught) engage, frustrate, and amuse. Their predicaments just seem to arrive, as a natural part of lived life. Her stories often feature tough topics, yes, but they are authentic, organically introduced, and full of surprise. If, for example, you'd told me I'd be reading a story that includes Heidegger, homelessness, drug addiction, and a middle-aged man living quietly in a residential neighborhood with his wife and child, *and* that I would be smiling at every turn, I'd have been doubtful at the very least. If you told me that, despite the heaviness of topics, I would be underlining and starring bright bits of language to savor later, I would have thought, *Highly unlikely.* But then, I had yet to read "Nightlight." I had yet to read any of the stories in this book, which out of a growing feeling of intimacy and affection I have come to nickname *Eight Legs*.

The fiction I love is not written to educate. I prefer to travel along with the characters, like cherished companions. If I learn, discover, or ponder ideas I might not have encountered prior to reading an author—great. But these eight short stories were earned, in a way that only comes over time. It is character, language, and feeling that count in Campbell's work. I wouldn't want it any other way.

ALICE SEBOLD, *The Lovely Bones*
Judge, Mary McCarthy Prize in Short Fiction
June 2020

THE MAN WITH EIGHT PAIRS OF LEGS

THE MAN WITH
EIGHT PAIRS OF LEGS

Cañon City was not a city. It was a small, gossiping, high-security town in Colorado's high desert, bordered to the west by the Sawatch Range. A home-rule municipality boasting thirteen prisons and fifty churches, its ten thousand people—one-fifth of them locked up—governed themselves as they saw fit and thrived on the stories, true or false, they told themselves.

Everyone in Cañon knew that thirty-four-year-old Harriet Rogers, the reclusive, six-foot-tall history teacher at Coolidge High, was not a drinker. Nor did she hang out in bars. But on this clear, wintry night, heading down Main Street toward the interstate, her Buick, like a stubborn horse, bucked and halted in front of Lola's Saloon of its own accord. Or at least that's how the town later came to explain it.

Harriet worked her lanky frame into a dark back booth and shrugged off her winter coat. The ceaseless swill of pandering speeches at the Christmas faculty dinner had driven her to near madness, her nerve endings lighting up randomly like rollovers, spinners, and kickers in pinball machines just below the skin. She had fled the cavernous gym, inadvertently releasing two green helium balloons into the night. She could still taste the sugary punch.

"Anything that burns," she called out to the bartender as she pulled a stack of midterms from her satchel. But the bartender, a middle-aged man coiffed in a slick, pink toupee, couldn't hear her over the half dozen regulars jostling at his trough—prison guards, farmers, and merchants—each one attempting to one-up the other with accounts of Cañon's breaking news. A rabid sheepdog up and chased down Litton's prize Appaloosa! You heard Old Dumbarton's cow got its head stuck in the homestead fence? Bet she was gunning for greener pastures . . .

"Get a load of this one," someone said. Harriet looked up to see an unfamiliar man in a motorcycle jacket position himself at the bar. "Giant fireball came out of nowhere," he said, taking off his jacket and mimicking the thrust of the thing with his arm. "Pure methane."

The locals fell silent. The bartender set down the collins glass he'd been wiping with a towel.

"Happened over at Buckhorn Mine in Gunnison a few years back," the young man said. "I saw the whole thing. Sucked out the oxygen so fast, sixteen men died in an instant before it exploded at a boy's feet."

Harriet leaned in. Fatalities soothed her the way frightening fairy tales soothe children because it's not happening to them. She lit a cigarette, deeply inhaling the pleasure, then exhaled uneasily when the young man noticed her from across the bar and headed to her table. He wasn't a big man, but he walked like one.

"Callahan," he said, by way of introduction. His dark hair was greased, rolled back from his brow like a scroll. Harriet felt the heat on her legs from the clicking wall radiator beneath her table. Like a fool, she relit her lit cigarette. He slid the stack of exams to the side and bought her two shots of exactly what she'd ached for. She must have winced.

"I take it you're not a regular," he said, joining her in the booth. "Me neither."

She glanced at him, then, from behind the curtain of her hair, surprised by the genuine tenderness in his voice. He was younger than her, and shorter, his broad shoulders pushing against blue flannel. It was the nineties, not the seventies, but he punched in John Denver, "Rocky Mountain High," and led her to the small, straw-strewn square beneath sagging Christmas lights, where, even hunched, she towered over him, his head resting against her mannish chest. After last call, she expected him to vanish, but he followed her on his motorcycle, eerie in her taillights, past the soaring pylons of Royal Gorge Bridge—its multistrand cables edged with snow—and out into the prairie.

No man had kissed Harriet since a male colleague at Coolidge cornered her in the locker room five years before. But Callahan did. He craned his neck and they kissed in the narrow hallway in front of Grandma Lily's crucifixes, and sepia portraits of Lily's mother and sisters, buttoned-up and bodiced like Gold Rush pioneers. Callahan laid her down on her bed and undressed her—first her coat, then her wrinkle-free pantsuit jacket and blouse, carefully lifting out her arms. With a single finger he traced her collarbones, along the borders of her no-nonsense bra before unbuttoning her slacks. His chapped hands, warm on her skin, held the ravages of winter. The sensation alarmed her—her body, the nicked mannequin she washed, dressed, put to bed, and sometimes forgot to feed, suddenly surging with blood. In the quiet of her grandmother's farmhouse, she could hear it, like creeks beneath the snow, a muted rushing sound.

Callahan, half naked, smelled like tree bark after rain. Harriet breathed him in as he molded her hips and legs with his hands, granting her a shapeliness she knew for a fact she didn't have. In her groin, a small muscle beat like a baby bird. With his fingers he entered her, a wet hollowing, as if he craved what she held there. She should have warned him: there was nothing. Yet suddenly there it was—an excruciating pleasure, a pleasure he knew just how to sustain.

Callahan moaned, or perhaps it had been she who had moaned, as she shimmied his jeans and boxers over his hips and broad upper thighs. She was about to tug them further, when they instead slid to the floor of their own accord and pooled around the ankles of his cowboy boots. She cried out—she didn't mean to, but Callahan had no legs. Black plastic cups screwed into what looked like majorette batons. She closed the curtains without thinking—no houses for miles in any direction.

Keeping his eyes on her, he pulled off the snug socket that attached to his left thigh. A tiny sucking sound escaped as the seal broke and released the stump, swaddled in its nylon sock. She grabbed a sweatshirt off a hook. He did the same thing with his right, then grimaced as he slowly rolled off each sock, exposing what remained of his thighs, drawn in at the stub, the stumps round and smooth as peeled potatoes. She could barely look at him as he swiveled his torso farther back onto her bed, leaving his metal legs crosshatched on the floor, boots still attached.

"I was sixteen," he said.

"That was you?" But she could see the anguish now in his eyes, behind the gentleness, darker than the collapsed mine itself, too painful to look at.

"The diamond-bit drill that could have saved my legs came too late."

From her seat in the booth at the bar, Harriet had heard the gruesome details. Hours after the explosion, rescuers had found the wounded boy bleeding in the tunnel, both his legs mangled, one foot tossed off to the side still in its boot. She had pitied the dutiful kid shearing coal so he could buy a fishing pole or, perhaps, a bracelet for his sweetheart, upset that he had not been in school, certain he was dead.

"Why didn't you say something?" she asked, confounded by dueling images: the thrilling raconteur at the bar who'd just seduced her and this contrite, disabled man. She had never known an amputee, had certainly never seen one without clothes.

"I wouldn't be here with you now," he said. He pulled Lily's quilt over his thighs.

"You don't have to do that," she said. "You really don't." But she was careful not to touch him when she joined him on her bed.

Neither spoke. Like a pantomime, they navigated their bodies into the sheets. Lying down, it was the dull weight of her own long-limbed body she felt pressing down like stone into the mattress.

The summer before fourth grade, Harriet had shot up like prairie grass. For years, she became the butt of every child's joke. *Is it cold up there?* they would ask. In high school, her classmates ridiculed her—the girls as much as the boys—for her awkward walk, for being *flatter than a baking sheet*. She still carried that hurt, a stillborn wedged inside her. Back then, she'd tried starving it, cutting into it with razors, scarring her thighs and wrists.

"Callahan," she heard herself say out loud, just to confirm he was really there.

"I still feel the pain in them," he confided.

He called them his phantoms, which made perfect sense. She'd searched, but had repeatedly failed to find the locus of her own indelible suffering, an ache that seemed to reach far beyond the bitterness still lingering from a childhood of mockery. And yet, if she paid attention to it, the pain seemed to spread everywhere, like miniature firing squads beneath her clothes. She started to tell him, but stopped herself.

They fell asleep without touching, but in the middle of the night, Harriet woke to the odd sensation of his thigh against hers, warmer than she expected. Frightened, she moved away but still felt something over there, pulsing and bloody, as if the legs blown off in Gunnison were in her sheets. She slid her hand to where they should have been, but there was nothing there.

———

The next morning, Harriet watched Callahan transfer himself to the floor in one swift motion and zip down the hall to the bathroom, pushing his naked torso forward with his hands, his stumps extended in front of him, before reappearing bedside, shameless and smooth like some mythic creature. His ungreased hair fell into his eyes, making him look even younger than he was.

"I'd like it if you let me stay," he said, rubbing his shoulders against the cold. "But not out of pity."

Nimble as a skier, he reattached his limbs. Molded feet that would never blister—permanently ensconced in cowboy boots—were secured to silver pipes that connected, just above the metal knee joints, to thigh sockets pale as a mannequin's, each one fitting snugly over its stump like a thimble on a thumb. His legs, destined until the end of time to be free of varicose veins, were effortlessly fastened to his torso in seconds, at which point, crouching on all fours, his hands close to his chest, he pushed himself up with his arms so that his body took the shape of a V, then he walked his prosthetic legs to his hands and stood up, assembled and strong in front of her. He brushed his hair back with both hands, his transformation nothing short of miraculous.

It wasn't pity Harriet felt, nor the confusion she'd felt the night before. It was envy.

"I'd like you to stay," she said.

He looked at her, and she at him, like mule deer on the prairie once the hunters are gone. She opened the curtains, forgetting that her own pilloried body, along with its latticework of scars, would be exposed to the salt-light of day. Outside, Mount Elbert rose up over fourteen thousand feet, majestic above stratus clouds; below, the wide, white prairie unblemished by footprints.

Callahan relaxed against the headboard of her bed.

"Tell me about yourself," he said, a solicitation she hadn't heard since Grandma Lily died. He waited, looking at her as if his life might depend on what she was about to say.

"My mom lives in town. I miss her. We rarely talk." Harriet's words poured out.

She and Fay had always been close, she told him. But when her mother married Rick Paden, the salacious town barber, twenty years ago, and gave birth to two insolent boys, she had escaped here to her grandmother's farm where Lily, in her modest way, had done her best to assuage her bouts of torment by simply listening to her, her small hand on Harriet's arm.

Now Lily, too, was gone. At the wake last year, Harriet had reached into the coffin to loosen the tight straps on her grandmother's Sunday pumps. She'd rubbed off rouge, messed up the dead woman's lacquered hair. "Look what they've done to her!" she'd said. "Let her rest, Harriet," Fay had pleaded, her own hair—Rick's hobby in his afterhours—dyed platinum and sprayed into a helmet as if crafted by Lily's mortician. "Please," she had said. "Let us all rest."

"The woman in the coffin wasn't Lily," Harriet told Callahan. "How could I say goodbye?"

Harriet thought she should stop there. She had already said

too much. But Callahan, having responded to her every word with a raised eyebrow or a sympathetic tilt of the head, gestured for her to continue—as if she, Harriet Rogers, were the most interesting person.

Without her students, she told him, she might not have survived in Cañon City. She fell in love with them each year, the curious no more than the recalcitrant. In a school where evolution was folklore, she refused to use state-sanctioned textbooks, instead plastering her classroom with copies of original documents she'd tracked down and old letters written by ordinary people. At graduation, sitting in the back of the auditorium, listening to her seniors read the hopeful, honest speeches she'd encouraged them to write, her heart would break each time, as if they were already gone. Then, each September, the chairs would fill up again with brashness and innocence, cotton-candy lip gloss and acne.

She told him how much she treasured the high prairie, how she couldn't bear not to wake every day to the Sawatch Range out her windows, that some of her best moments had been spent on their slopes, veering off Forest Service trails, listening to the hum of time.

Callahan nodded, *hmmming* and *mmming* little sounds of recognition and pleasure, as if he actually understood.

"My mom died young," he told her when she finished talking. "After that, my dad moved to Billings."

Callahan had no siblings. Before the mining accident, he'd been a runner. Since coming to Cañon City, he'd been squatting in an abandoned trailer in Temple Park. Last week, he'd been hired as a day cook at the ADX, the Alcatraz of the Rockies.

"The prisoners *beg* me to show up in shorts," he said, grinning. "When I do, they slap me on the back. 'Bro, I'd rather get life' they like to tease. 'Prison suddenly doesn't seem so bad!'"

"I'm picturing security," Harriet said, surprised that she, of all people, was planning to tell a joke. "The guy manning the conveyor belt is standing in his uniform. He's not smiling. He's bored. Items pass by: keys, watches, oh my god! A pair of legs!"

Callahan's laughter pitched into the room, the most delightful sound.

"They use a hand scanner," he said. "They let you keep your legs."

Then he stroked the length of her body as if it were made of silk. His hands felt different now, not like the disembodied foragers or gloves on fire she had felt last night, but a real man's hands. At first, the sensation was frightening, as if he'd located her phantom body, the one she'd been hiding even from herself.

Callahan didn't leave that day, or the day after. Hemmed in by winter, there was really no place to go. He made love to her, and she to him. They tried unconventional positions, with and without his prosthetics, sometimes holding each other so tightly Harriet thought there must be a steep precipice on either side. If he noticed her scars, he didn't say. Through the bedroom window, they watched his Harley-Davidson disappear under drifts of snow.

———

Callahan, it turned out, had been hiding more than his aluminum legs. Over breakfast, he confessed he'd come to Cañon City to compete in the Human Race, a one-mile foot race that had been added, after much debate in the Chamber of Commerce the prior year, to the Fremont County Fair's time-honored Tractor Race, Hog Race, and Pinewood Derby—which seemed preposterous. Harriet, of course, knew about the annual fair's obsession with perfection: blue-ribbon pigs and cows, prize-winning apples and cakes. She'd gone every May as a child. Her own immaculate mother repeatedly won the baking contest with her four-layer jam pies. Harriet couldn't imagine how, with his baton legs, Callahan could run at all, much less run a race.

"In a wheelchair?" she ventured to ask. She pictured a herd of Iraq vets jostling into each other's wheels as they set off around the track, knowing that Cañon, hogtied by tradition, was not prepared to add a Paralympics to their fair.

"You're not getting it, Harriet," he said. "Look, there's something I need you to understand. It took two years for me to even walk on these sticks; five more to be able to jog without falling. Even with the Buckhorn settlement, it took forever to afford running blades so I wouldn't have to give up everything I loved."

"Blades? For running?" Callahan kept shape-shifting in front of her.

"I'm fast," he said. "I want to run against your able-bodied men."

It was a long shot—the parochial Chamber of Commerce

would never let him run. Even if they did, he was a squatter, not a resident. She knew the rules.

"They won't let you compete without a Fremont address," she told him, surprised to find herself retrieving her extra house key from a kitchen drawer and placing it in his hand, then giving his prosthetic knee a conspiratorial squeeze, which she immediately realized he couldn't feel.

Callahan showed up at Harriet's place the next day, the back of his motorcycle loaded with a duffel bag of clothes, mountaineering equipment, and three pairs of the most fascinating legs Harriet had ever seen. If she'd been insecure about his motives, she no longer cared. Callahan lined them up in a row like golf clubs against her bedroom wall and introduced them to her. Each pair had its own name.

To climb mountain faces, he wore the metal Sharmas with their small titanium feet that fit so nicely into fissures. The green waterproof Hoogenbands had wide, webbed fins that had allowed him to swim in the Gunnison River. His curved black Flex-Foot pair, the Cheetahs, were the ones that gave him spring and speed—their carbon fiber J-shaped feet, which compressed to store energy and then release it, had been modeled after a cheetah's hind legs. Not one of them was a cosmetic replacement for what had gone missing—designed, instead, to match whatever he wished to achieve.

His legs were expensive, but Callahan, by volunteering for university research trials, got them from a company in Iceland

for a discount. His silver day-to-day pair, the ones he was wearing, he called his Two Buck Chucks. He'd put every penny he
earned into his prosthetics.

His fifth pair, Callahan told her, was a secret. A week after he
moved in, he surprised her by wearing them to bed. She rubbed
her calves against their red velvet skin, undeniably softer and
more erotic than her own. Callahan called them his Casanovas.
Harriet's lackluster bedroom suddenly looked like her vision of
an edgy art gallery in Chicago or New York.

Over the next few weeks, Harriet and Callahan settled into a
daily routine. He went to his job cooking at the ADX. She went
to Coolidge High where lockdowns were routine due to the recent
Columbine massacre just miles away, and frequent prisoner
escapes. They had dinner. Callahan trained at twilight, when
no one was out. On weekends, if they weren't taking a walk
on the plowed highway or discussing Harriet's latest pedagogic
provocation on Lily's glassed-in porch—*what if a Cherokee woman
had been the seventh president instead of Jackson*, she would ask her
students. *Would there still have been a Trail of Tears? What if the
Yankees had lost the Civil War?*—they were making love in the
different rooms of Lily's house, even venturing into the chilly
toolshed and barn.

Here with this man, touched in parts she didn't know she
had, Harriet's comatose limbs and torso were waking. But
with the waking came the shame. Not even Lily had been able
to understand the relentless daily battle she'd had to wage to

contain the clandestine life of her body, one hundred and forty pounds of bone and nerve endings, blood cells circulating like tiny milk trucks delivering oxygen, her indefatigable heart pumping ninety beats per minute, the body she hadn't chosen, and that, by the age of ten, she'd chosen to reject. Ever since high school, she'd repudiated all accessories and makeup, worn unstylish clothes. The largest women's sizes, longer in the arms, legs, and waist, were still too short, and inevitably loose on her lean frame.

One Sunday afternoon after lovemaking in the barn, Harriet brushed the straw from her hot, vibrating skin, in awe of her own body. Outside, the wind throttled the old barn walls. Callahan slept peacefully next to her beneath a woolen stable-blanket. Harriet tried to calm herself, but her heart refused to stop pumping every bridled schoolyard insult back into her blood. As if propelled by ghosts, she ran naked through the snow until she was standing in front of the only mirror she allowed in the house. There it was, her visible body—nipples like peach pits spit onto the pavement; a platter of ribs; arms, loose pickets on a fence. She couldn't see her legs in the small mirror, but her face was there, unremarkable, even obsequious.

That night, Callahan's torso spooning her in bed, she wondered if she needed a man to be disfigured in order to let him love her.

Throughout that winter, Callahan talked constantly about progress in prosthetics technology. If what he envisioned didn't exist, he did his best to design it. She found paper napkins, even Kleenex, inked up with his amateur diagrams and scribbled notations. Biomedical engineers at MIT had been working for three years on prosthetics, he told her, that would allow people like him to feel temperature and pressure in their lower limbs. He received occasional updates. They were getting close.

Meanwhile, Harriet's human legs felt increasingly burdensome and deficient. In the cold, they ached. At night, they felt gangly, bone-heavy. Running behind Callahan one Saturday, out of breath, falling farther behind each minute but refusing to give up, she'd ended up in bed icing her shin splints. Harriet found herself coveting each new innovation as much as Callahan did. If only she could snap on her own Cheetahs and sprint by his side.

One afternoon, when he was still at work, she dragged out Lily's full-length mirror, which she had hidden in a closet, and leaned it against her bedroom wall. She pulled over a chair, loaded it with encyclopedias, and knelt on top so she could hold the Sharmas and the Casanovas to her knees like real legs, to see how they would look. They looked magnificent, sleek and otherworldly. She began designing her own artificial limbs in her head, fabulous legs, six inches shorter than her own, synthetic legs that would, like Callahan's, rid her of the bane of aging, but also the curse of height, a pair molded from Venetian glass, another with her favorite cowboy boots permanently attached.

That evening, her head on Callahan's lap, she told him about her fantasy. He just laughed.

"And I think I'll trade my head in for a new one!" he said. "How about Ben Stiller?"

But her proposition had been serious.

"We could be immortal," she told him. "Just you and I."

"I adore your mortal legs," he said.

Harriet relished her weeks of privacy with Callahan, but they didn't last. Once the snow began melting, he no longer waited until dark to run. He began training weekends. The spectacle of him sprinting in his Cheetahs along the gorge became a familiar sight, inspiring awe, but also uneasiness, in the town. Rumors abounded. People talked in the post office and on street corners. The butcher confided in the priest and the priest confided in the woman who made candles, the scuttlebutt reaching a crescendo at Rick's barbershop on Main. Perhaps it was the strange beauty of Callahan's stride, or the ugliness of a human-machine, or simply the incongruence of *amputee* and *speed*. It was something none of them had seen before. They just couldn't seem to explain their feelings of apprehension. The news—that this odd, yet oddly attractive, *freak from Gunnison* aimed to challenge real men with real legs in the one-mile at the Human Race—divided Cañon City like an apple wrenched in two by bare hands.

Wearing Cheetahs in a footrace is like Mercury wearing his wingeð sanðals, the principal at Coolidge High opined in an editorial in the *Cañon Bee*. *But we are not goðs; we are men.*

Of course, there were also many who decried the small-mindedness of the outspoken few, arguing at water coolers *to let the poor kid run*. No one really knew anything about Callahan, not like Harriet did. They gossiped and dreamed, each one fashioning their idea of him out of their own secret fears and yearnings.

On Valentine's Day, Harriet returned from school to find Callahan setting the table wearing a short terry robe and his Two Buck Chucks, looking, even to her, like science fiction. He set a steaming plate of grilled trout and Rocky Mountain oysters in front of her, along with a single red rose in a jam jar. But when she kissed him, he barely kissed her back.

"I'm a person," he said, "not a fucking impairment. Why can't this town just leave me alone?"

"They're afraid you'll win," she said.

"It's not about winning."

He put his napkin in his lap and they ate in silence, the only sound the ticking of Lily's kitchen clock. Halfway through the meal, he scooted back his chair. His countenance had changed.

"I have a surprise for you," he said.

He left the room and came back ten minutes later five inches taller, dramatically ducking under the door frame, wearing a faux-Armani suit. When he lifted her from her chair, he was an inch taller than her. She couldn't help it, but had to turn from him so he wouldn't see her tears. He spun her around. She didn't have to bend into his embrace. She smelled the Listerine on his breath.

"They came yesterday," he whispered in her ear. "My Mings." He pulled up both pant legs to display his perfectly shaped peach-colored calves and knees.

"We can go dancing," he said. "You can wear your heels."

It was as if his sixth pair of legs had subsumed every previous affront or slur. As if, in that moment, Cañon City had disappeared. But it also made him forget who *she* was. Harriet was not a woman who wore heels. Just yesterday, at the faculty Valentine's lunch, her ungainly legs had been cramped beneath the low school-district table while her female colleagues, decked out like baubles in bright-colored blazers with matching skirts, had laughed and scoffed and crossed their legs with ease, raising their Dixie cups like ballet dancers as if they'd been graced. Callahan's Mings would not change that. He could be tall, but she could never be short. Even if she could, her wounds would still be there. Even now, her network of nerves buzzed beneath her pantsuit like ripped electric wire.

"It's not what I want," she said.

Callahan took off his suit jacket and sat back down at the table. The trout was cold.

"At least, I can dunk with the best of them," he said, "at the prison gym."

Harriet looked for the flicker of light she'd seen in his eyes when he'd left the room, for any sign of the tenderness she so often saw there, but could only see his pain. This time, she didn't look away. How stupid she'd been, fantasizing about hitching on her own glorious legs sculpted from glass or velvet. She knew only too well that the life of a double amputee was far from glorious. There were the lidocaine patches Callahan had to use twice a day to numb the place where his prosthetics attached to his stumps, the gabapentin for the bone spurs, the desipramine for the excruciating neuromas.

She got up from the table, unhitched his Mings, and laid them on the floor. Lightly, the way he liked it, she massaged the cross-stitch scars that traversed his residual limbs. Tomorrow, when he walked out the door, he would once again be objectified, marveled at and scorned. In hair salons and bars, the endless speculations about the two of them would continue: "The man shacking up with the maverick history teacher has six pairs of legs, fifteen pairs, twenty-five," the number always increasing. No one said anything about love.

But that's what it was.

"We have to be patient," she said. That's what Lily had always told her when Harriet's sorrow wouldn't quit. Out on the porch, where they could see the imposing silhouette of the Sawatch, her grandmother would recount the legend of how Cañon's Royal Gorge had been made, a small stream of melting snow from Mount Elbert cutting through granite, one foot every 2,500 years, until it completely severed Fremont Peak. The story always soothed Harriet's restlessness. In fact, she'd passed the remedy along to her students, pitting their angst and volatility against Precambrian history, which they too found comforting.

"You know I can't quit," he said. "You understand that."

The sun had set. Together, they moved to the window and watched the greening world soften. Two hawks glided in and out of wind currents over the fields.

"Someday that will be you and me," Harriet said. "With implanted wings."

By late March, just as spring lambs began falling from their ewes, a sea change occurred in the high desert. The naysayers of Cañon had grown accustomed to Callahan's surreal silhouette, a blur along the gorge. While there were still those who secretly harbored a perverse, unacknowledged desire to witness *a presumptuous man's humiliation*, one could feel the town's desire to witness the impossible—Callahan running against their men in the Human Race. Everyone seemed to agree: the event would be more entertaining than anything that had happened in Cañon in years. Dozens rallied in front of City Hall for the mayor and the Chamber of Commerce to allow Callahan to run. The prisoners Callahan cooked for at the ADX xeroxed flyers and bribed the prison guards to hand them out, their enthusiasm helping to sway the town in Callahan's favor.

A week before Easter vacation, Harriet stopped at the drugstore on Main Street to pick up Callahan's painkiller prescriptions. Having doubled his training time, he required a double dose. In front of her at checkout, the mayor, a short, heavyset man, who had dated Harriet's mother Fay before Rick had swept her off her feet, was buying a pair of sunglasses.

He turned from the cashier, gesturing for Harriet to bend down to his height.

"The conservative bastards met last night," he whispered,

referring to the Chamber. "They tore at each other's throats like jackals. But they finally agreed. Callahan can run. Mum's the word. They'll announce it publicly in a couple of weeks."·

"Oh my god!" she said, as he gave her a surreptitious high five below the counter.

The vote felt like Harriet's victory, too, an affirmation here in her own backyard. It's the nickels and dimes that make history, she always told her students, not the hundred-dollar bills. She couldn't wait to tell Callahan.

"If I were a cripple, I'd stay in my house where I belonged," the cashier said, slapping down the mayor's change with so much vitriol three pennies rolled to the floor.

Callahan, of course, felt vindicated by the news. He added Parkdale, a small town thirteen miles away, to his daily training course, sprinting and jogging in intervals. He ran before dawn, after work, on weekends. In his eagerness to prove himself, he forgot about the prospect of the MIT legs and his desire, Harriet assumed, to feel her heat. He started skipping dinner, catching a bite instead at the ADX. He was becoming more sinewy, smaller in the waist.

Harriet did her best to remain upbeat. But she missed their slow, secluded times together.

"Just two more months," he reassured her. "You have to be patient." He smiled. "A foot, remember? Every 2,500 years?"

On Tax Day, a seventh pair of legs arrived. Harriet watched as Callahan lifted them from the box. They were beautiful—too beautiful—as light as spoons with nylon snowshoes permanently attached. He named the new pair his Messners after the famous Everest mountaineer and lined them up with the others against her bedroom wall.

"I can hike your mountain with you," he said.

Callahan was courting her with his legs. She should have been pleased he wanted to be with her in the quiet places she most loved. But a groundswell of foreboding looted the thrill. She pictured herself bending over to put on three pairs of socks, pulling up waterproof pants, painstakingly strapping her unwieldy snowshoes, one to each foot, then traipsing through untrodden snow, Callahan ahead of her, his legs agile and numb to the cold, not freezing like hers.

That Sunday, they put chains on Harriet's tires and parked in a plowed empty lot at the base of her favorite trail. From here, she led Callahan onto the slopes of Mount Elbert. He was clumsy, at first, with his Messners, even with ski poles, attempting to follow in her footsteps as instructed by the warning sheet that came with the new prosthetics. She had to slow down repeatedly so he could keep pace with her, turning back to steady him when he was about to fall. Sunlight glistened on the new snow, and the sky, shot through with cobalt, hung low as if protecting them from whatever was on the other side. More than once she asked him to stop and listen to the immense quiet, a silence that seemed to swell. Her legs and feet were cold and damp, just as she'd feared. But here she was, alone with Callahan in the birthplace of the world.

Harriet wished the moment could go on forever. But early spring powder had already begun falling in tufts from the pines. The Human Race was just weeks away. Summer would come, then another winter. Callahan, having achieved his mission, would leave her.

She looked back at him. Snowflakes clung erratically to his red beanie. He smiled, stoically, his lips blue, his eyes serene. She loved this man, who, with his attentive hands, had given her back her body, a burden she could hardly bear. She closed her eyes, felt the icy air on her cheeks. In her mind, she saw Lily wearing the nightgown she wore when the two of them used to sit together talking late into the night, a sheer rayon that had, over the years, afforded Harriet a view of her own future deterioration—sag, flab, and waning sinew. There was no reason for it, but tears welled up anyway, a few pocking the surface of the snow.

"We won't last," she said, turning to Callahan. She pictured the two of them as if from a Cessna, tiny specks on the mountain. "Nothing human ever lasts."

"You're making me crazy," he said. "You really are. Even here in your favorite place, on this perfect day—look how gorgeous it is—you still have to build your own private city of suffering?" He touched a gloved hand to her brow. "It's not real, Harriet. It's all in here."

But her pain *was* real, as real as their footprints in the snow. She thought he'd understood. She tried to contain it, but her bruised heart refused to stay in its chamber, hurtling like a speeding train toward a mountain before the tunnel's been carved out.

"Everyone in Cañon knows about your injury," she said. "You just stand up and they applaud. But what about mine? I can't just ask some surgeon to cut it away, then conveniently replace it with something spectacular."

"That's not a fair comparison," he said, unzipping his snow pants and letting them drop to the elastic cuffs where his ankles should have been. "Fucking look at me!" He struck one of his Messners with his ski pole. It pinged, a tiny unnatural sound. "Sometimes I think all you care about is these. Would you have even let me stay if I hadn't had my fucking legs blown off?"

He swung at a pine, then took off his glove and swung again at the bark. His fist wasn't immortal. It was bleeding. It was as if he wanted it to bleed.

Harriet's racing heart crashed into the mountain. She grabbed at his jacket, but he escaped her grasp, pulled up his pants, and clomped away through the snow, more steadily now, as if his anger had solidified his center of gravity.

"We're not gods," she yelled after him. But he didn't turn around, even to fight.

Harriet didn't move. She couldn't. The Sawatch so still. And all their human hurt. And what about him? If he had been an able-bodied man, would he have ever sauntered over and bought her a drink in the first place? Where does the diminishment start? she wondered, love by default, by last resort. She watched her boyfriend disappear through the trees, first the back of his jacket, then his beanie, just a fleck of red.

Alone on her mountain, Harriet felt something in her gut, a

kind of settling, like dirt that's found its way to the bottom of the pond. She'd told Callahan the truth and Mount Elbert, like a good teacher, had listened. Standing now at eight thousand feet, she felt her own rootedness, as if there were a plumb line from her heart to the earth's core.

But the mountain soon darkened—a cluster of clouds eclipsed the sun, a possible storm. She remembered the warnings: *A snow-drift's depth is unpredictable,* the manual had said. *Never navigate alone.* Callahan could be in danger, buried in snow even now, unable to get up on his own. Harriet set out in the direction he'd gone, but her snowshoes slowed her down. She took them off, scrambling over rocky mounds and fallen limbs, following Callahan's tracks in her three layers of socks. But the tracks vanished. Panicked, she called his name. No answer. *Callahan! Callahan!* The sensation of him being gone, truly gone, seared through her like a welder's torch. She couldn't feel her feet. Again and again, she called for him as she clambered down the mountain's slope until she reached the parking lot, where she found him huddled in the passenger seat of her Buick, his Messners, still inside their snow pants, tossed into the back, his jacket lining wrapped like a blanket around his stumps.

Harriet spent that night in her bed with a towel and a pot of hot water attending to her frostbite, until she could feel her feet again, while Callahan slept soundly under Lily's quilt on the living room couch. When she woke, he was gone.

That afternoon, returning from Coolidge, she stopped in

Cañon to pick up his pain pill refills, then walked outside to the street she'd known since she was born. The sky above the low buildings was rain-washed blue. She walked past the old Owl Cigar Store with its wooden booths and long line of red-and-silver stools along the counter; past her stepfather's loud and crowded barbershop smelling of chemical dyes and lemon aftershave; past the historic three-story Hotel St. Cloud on the corner. Lola's looked dark and cool inside with a gaggle of early drinkers around the bar. The town she'd hated to love. None of it looked real, a phantom town.

In the twin plate glass doors of the State Armory, Harriet caught sight of her reflection. The woman in the glass was not nearly as unattractive as she felt. The deep-set eyes radiated tiny rays of light that skittered, dreamlike, across the surface. The cheeks looked unnaturally pink like the rouged Tall Woman who had come to town with the traveling circus when Harriet was a young child, before the bullying, and the licentious barber, when Harriet had still been enamored by her own body. She watched, entranced, the edges of her reflection slowly blurring into the dark interior of the Armory lobby. An encroaching shadow soon began to eat away at the delicate woman who stared back at her—first the head and arms, then the torso and legs—until the sun had set behind the building across the street, and her reflection vanished.

Harriet wanted Callahan to notice the pretty woman she'd discovered by chance, but since their hike on the mountain, he kept to himself. She taught her American History classes with her usual fervor, but couldn't get the dreaded prophecy out of her head: her lover's legs no longer leaning against her bedroom wall, Callahan back at the abandoned trailer in Temple Park. But Callahan stayed, grim and determined, concentrating on his training course. One evening, as she was reading diary entries from indentured servants for her next day's lesson, he surprised her, coming home early from the ADX, even kissing her on the cheek, then giving her a wink before leaving again with his Cheetahs. That he would be allowed to run in the Human Race was still their secret.

But on the last day of April, the Chamber announced their decision in the *Cañon Bee* and draped a hand-painted banner— MR. CALLAHAN CAN RUN!—over the front railing of City Hall, which drove the citizenry of Cañon to near distraction. The next day, the *Bee* published an interview along with a photo: Callahan wearing nothing but shorts and Cheetahs, running at sunset by the gorge. A Denver paper picked it up and within a week calls started to come in, first the small counties like Pitkin, Elbert, Yuma and Archuleta, then larger ones like Mesa and Pueblo, requesting that Callahan race in their county fairs. They would cut through red tape, they promised, and establish their own Human Races. Along his training route, a band of high school girls took to screaming as he passed by, staging histrionic swoons. The boys seemed to venerate the superpowers of their very own 3-D Bionic Man. One group of Coolidge girls got fake tattoos with Callahan's name, which they openly displayed as the weather warmed. To Harriet's horror, Callahan, who'd begun sleeping with her again, their hearts mending, seemed to relish the attention, jogging into town and sprinting down Main Street to wave at his fans, teenyboppers and shopkeepers, then bragging about it at dinner.

The hysteria went on like this for days.

One evening, the fair a couple weeks away, Callahan came home late after an afternoon interval run to Coal Creek. Harriet woke to find him standing over her, his wet hair matted against his brow. She was surprised to smell beer on his breath. He never drank while training. He must have stopped at Lola's.

"I'm going to win!" he said, as if this were a rebuttal to an argument, and grabbed her wrist so tight it hurt.

"Of course," she said. She had never seen him drunk. But every night after that, he came home later, more intoxicated, jeopardizing his training. When she asked him about it, he didn't answer. But each morning, as he rose from bed before dawn, she heard him curse under his breath. From the living room window, she watched him tie his Cheetahs onto the back of his motorcycle and screech onto the highway, frightened for his safety.

Mid-May, the editor of the *Cañon Bee* made a radical prediction in his Sunday column that shocked the town: *Over the next few decades, nascent technologies will transform life not only for the impaired, but also for the healthy, who will find hearing what they have never heard, seeing what they have never seen, remembering what they never remember, and running faster than they have ever run, irresistible.*

Harriet, alone at the breakfast table with the paper, wanted to discuss the editorial with Callahan, but he was never there. The following evenings and weekend, she paced alone through Lily's empty rooms. Fay's perfect hair, the bartender's slicked-back strawberry toupee, fake eyelashes and rouge—these were superficial enhancements, ones she'd refused, even held in disdain. But there were other options, transformative choices that went far beyond accessories invented for the dead and the vain.

Haven't we always added to ourselves? she thought. Imitating birds with hang-gliding wings and parachutes, designing ourselves for the ice and snow; roller skates and oxygen tanks deep in the sea; high heels for calf lines, tap shoes for the percussive racket; pogo sticks and stilts. Might we one day really implant wings?

On Monday, she pulled into the Coolidge High School parking lot like a sorceress in her old Buick and read the controversial editorial to her students. "What would *you* do," she asked them, "if given the choice to alter yourselves? Would you be loyal? Wouldn't you keep the bodies you've been given at birth?" But nearly every one of them, girls and boys alike, said they'd do whatever it took to be smarter, stronger, better. They were teenagers, after all, figuring out who they even were in the world. Their video game characters bored them to tears if they didn't have godlike powers like shape-shifting or telekinesis.

"I wasn't born with this perm, Ms. Rogers," a girl said, coyly turning her head to the boy behind her. "Turquoise contact lenses!" "Nose jobs!" "Steroids!" her students called out.

Harriet, disturbed by their audaciousness, quickly recognized that it had partly been her doing. Hadn't she spent the entire year empowering them with copies of letters from maids who became pilots, orphans who reached the North Pole, housewives who cleaned up oil spills? She had put their birthdays up on the history timeline that stretched from wall to wall above the chalkboard, right there with Johannes Gutenberg and the Magna Carta, to remind them that they, not the men and women deified by textbooks, were the makers of history.

"You're deluding them," the principal had accused her at a faculty meeting. "You're inflating their significance!"

"What about heart transplants?" Harriet asked the thirty seniors now in front of her. "Would you take out a perfectly good heart if you thought another one was better?" She could hear a pin drop. The sun, having finally risen above Pikes Peak, streamed through the eastern windows, brightening their rapt faces, but also marking them with shadow.

"What about perfectly good legs?" she asked.

Then the door swung open and the principal popped his bald head in, shiny as a minted coin, which put an end to all discussion.

That evening, Callahan out running, Harriet felt her body so keenly, it terrified her: its relentless pulse and weight, but also its transience. She could feel each cell disintegrating, every vein coursing with loneliness. She heated up the chicken and pasta Callahan had prepared for her before settling on the sofa in Lily's glassed-in porch to watch the first spring thunderstorm crawl across the prairie. Random bolts of lightning crackled over the land, lighting up the vast darkness. Callahan, she was sure, was out there somewhere, soaking wet, jogging and sprinting. Nothing, it seemed, could stop him from his training.

At nine o'clock, the storm knocked the electricity out. She got up and lit a candle before sitting back down with the pack of cigarettes Callahan had hidden from her behind cans of soup. Whatever it was that was growing inside her felt urgent; the urgency, pernicious. Anyone with half a mind would do whatever it took to be smarter, stronger, better. She understood that. But what might they do for love? Callahan had ordered his Mings and Messners to be closer to her. Why should she wait for decades? She pictured them now, both double amputees, on the front of *Time* magazine, fourteen pairs of the most magnificent legs lined up behind them—finally, inextricably, together.

Over the next few days, the image grew more tantalizing and vivid. She considered the way the mind can step into another world with its own parameters. How these new constraints build within themselves a kind of compulsion to do the most horrible thing. She already had cuts on her thighs, the old scars like a dotted line. It was madness, but at different times during the day, the madness took over, the sensation intensifying each time Callahan left the house. She was reminded of protestors who immolated themselves for a cause, the courage it takes. At the market, she steered herself away from buying practice bones from the butcher, scaring herself as the compulsion persisted.

That night, she dreamt she and Callahan were alone in the living room during an electrical storm, Callahan napping without his prosthetics on the couch. Everything in the dream felt like an emergency: running to the barn in the rain, hauling in Lily's backup generator, Callahan waking to the high-pitched buzz of the electric saw. He hurtled off the couch, swung and hopped on his hands, then scooted and rolled across the floor, desperate to reach her, to stop her. But it was too late. The dream repeated itself the following night, and then again. There was never any blood, just the sawed-off flesh and bone and a man in a baggy suit, like a vacuum cleaner salesman, knocking at the door with her Venetian glass.

On Memorial Day, Callahan hollered for her when the doorbell rang. She came running. A star-struck delivery man handed him a package: Callahan's eighth pair of legs, the MIT legs he'd dreamed about for years, two elegant calf-shaped machines made from copper-colored carbon jammed with microprocessors and sensors capable of receiving feedback one hundred times per second in order to detect subtle changes in the environment. Equipped with state-of-the-art hydraulic knees, the new legs screwed into shiny black Darth Vader sockets with black liners. Instead of ankles, silver cylinders held key-sized controllers that fit into two perfectly shaped silicon feet.

The MIT legs, with their electronic skin and long-life batteries would allow Callahan, for the first time since the explosion in the mine, to "feel" heat in his lower limbs.

"Put them on," Harriet begged.

"Slow down," he said. "These are machines, like computers or electric drills. I need to read the instructions." He read them out loud to her. He showed her the electrodes. Within days, he had had the tiny conductors implanted in his residual limbs.

A week later, together in bed, she felt the warmth of him next to her, head to toe, and, he told her, he could feel the heat of her calves and feet for the first time against his MIT ones. An eerie convergence, they agreed, of the phantom and the real. Callahan wept with sensation as he made love to her, then stayed close as if affixed to her body, pressing against her as she pressed back until he fell asleep in her arms, his hand resting like a warm lid on the shallow curve of her breast. How Harriet had ached for this—the intimacy neither of them had been able to draw or imagine.

The next morning, Callahan didn't wake before dawn, or strap his Cheetahs to his motorcycle. He stayed with Harriet in their bed wearing his new legs as the sun rose and turned Harriet's furniture into gold. He skipped his training.

"You were right, of course," he said, sitting up next to her against the headboard. "We're not gods . . . when I was a boy, I used to run everywhere, even in the house. I ran to the market for my mother. I ran down to the river just to feel the cool air on my face. In junior high, I ran the four-hundred, everything in my body circulating and hot. I loved the crack of the shot, lunging out of my starting blocks, that feeling against my chest when I busted through the tape. I felt it again those first few weeks running along the gorge at twilight. Sometimes I'd open my arms when I ran. I felt so free."

Harriet listened, her hand on his knee, which pulsed now against her palm.

"This past month, I lost myself, didn't I? All the hoopla. It was killing me. I hated to admit it, but I forgot what it felt like just to run. I've wanted that feeling again. Then last night, when I felt you, really felt you with my whole body, I didn't want anything else."

She slid down and turned until her cheek rested against his chest.

"It's not in your head," he said, his fingers tangling in her stringy hair. "It's real. If you feel it, it's real, Harriet."

His words entered her skin like carbon into leaves. She felt the light in her veins.

Harriet called in sick to the principal, Callahan to the warden, and it went on like this for days, peaceful and private, like their first nights together, the farmhouse surrounded by prairie grass, lush now with wildflowers, damp from a light spring rain. Harriet opened the windows, letting the curtains billow in the breeze, the heat and scent of late spring wafting into the rooms. Out her bedroom window, Mount Elbert rose into a cloudless sky. She was a tall, flat, scrawny woman. Her flimsy nightgown couldn't conceal that. Yet she felt comfortable in her own skin, the way she had as a young child on Crestmoor Road, her mother sitting on the edge of her bed, the two of them listening to the rain.

She breathed it all in, then went to the kitchen, past her prudish great-aunts, to brew coffee. She returned with a bowl of apricots on a tray and scooted close to Callahan so he would feel her heat. But she also felt her own body against him, the frantic delivery trucks slowing down, her heart beating softly in its cavity, the welcome weight of everything she was—teacher, daughter, lover—pressing into the mattress, the woman Callahan needed to feel whole.

Together, they named his eighth pair of legs his Callahans.

On the day of the fair, all of Fremont County would be waiting for Callahan, even a few lucky prisoners cuffed to security guards who had made a special request. In a makeshift press box, a handful of journalists from Denver and Pueblo would be standing at the ready, cameras and notepads in hand. But Callahan would not come, an absence the people of Cañon would never be able to explain. They might imagine him off to the side of the track, poised in his Cheetahs like a strange bird. Or try to conjure him crouched with the others before the gun went off, even picturing the blur of his blades speeding around the track. But that afternoon, when the gun went off, and their able-bodied men shot off their starting blocks, something had already changed inside them. They might stomp and yell from the bleachers for their son or brother to win, but beneath that zeal, too quiet for them to hear, an inexplicable sadness would enter them. So that by the time the Human Race was all said and done, and they had filed from the bleachers to buy prize-winning apples and taste homemade pies, they would feel the gravity of it, a peculiar longing, as if the future might never come.

Meanwhile, Harriet and Callahan, wearing his eighth pair of legs, dozed on and off through the morning.

"You're wearing your Harriets!" Callahan joked after one of their lovemaking sessions.

"I guess so," she said, playfully kicking his shin.

"Ouch!"

They both laughed. With bionic love came pain.

At noon, he sat up and announced he'd like to take her to Gunnison, to the site of what had once been Buckhorn Mine. She laid out his lidocaine and gabapentin on the kitchen counter. After dressing, he helped her onto his motorcycle in his Two Buck Chucks and they sped through the high desert. Harriet leaned into his back, tightening her grip around his waist, as if they were one person.

Before turning west onto Highway 50, Callahan pulled into Royal Gorge Bridge lookout, setting his boots down so they could take in the view. A few tourists were snapping photos. The 1,260-foot bridge looked white in the midday sunlight, its giant aluminum chains slung between castellated steel girders, marring the natural landscape, but beautiful, too, even exquisite, the Arkansas River a thousand feet below. Its construction in 1929 had seemed an impossible feat and yet here it was, the tallest suspension bridge in the world, linking what had taken three million years to sever.

THUNDER IN ILLINOIS

Mr. Evans, who still loves Mrs. Evans, has thought up a dozen ways to leave her. Some literal, like lifting off in a Hughes 500P stealth helicopter from their tar-spun roof in rural Bradley. Some figurative, like disappearing into the pages of a John le Carré novel, exhaling honeyed tobacco on the cruel sands of a British beach. On this June morning, however, Mr. Evans, still robust at sixty-two, sits across from a field of corn on the back porch of the house Mrs. Evans inherited from her parents, and has a revelation. Every year, this same fallow field valiantly shoots up stalks and crowns them with a profusion of golden tassels, only to lie strafed each winter. Death, he decides, is his only way out.

He certainly doesn't have the courage to take his own life. But after yesterday's test results—his white blood cell count is rapidly climbing—he is able to picture himself happily buried at the intersection of Hobbie and Brookmont, free, finally, of corrupt financial schemes, ill-fated Southeast Asian infrastructure projects, airplane food, and, most importantly, love and the manic duplicity of it.

But not until he wins the word game with Mrs. Evans.

———

Mrs. Evans is a fourth-grade teacher who thrives on winning games, including ones she makes up. One might say it is her métier. She'll stop at the Union 76 on her way home from Kankakee Elementary and if the black numbers at the gas pump don't line up perfectly when she releases the trigger, say with an even $40.00, not a penny more or less, she tries again for $41.00. Sometimes gas leaks onto her shoes.

The true contest though, the one Mrs. Evans has come to enjoy the most, is playing Bali, a word game, with Mr. Evans—two decks of lettered cards packed into a small red-and-blue box she unearthed on a liquidation table at Sears—a contest that ramped up considerably in the eighties when the couple were in their forties and their three wayward children had left Bradley. Mr. and Mrs. Evans had given a joint sigh of relief. They could be alone at last to play the game, which they did almost every Saturday night—or Friday if they had a party to go to or a bridge game set up for Saturday.

The years went by. Mr. Evans's widowed father, a cattle rancher, died in a senior home in Nebraska. Mrs. Evans's immigrant parents, haberdasher and housewife, were fleshless by now in their Waldheim graves. The Bali scores are cumulative. Mrs. Evans has always been in the lead, though there have been times when they were neck and neck for weeks. Then Mrs. Evans would put down a game stopper like *quixotic* or *xenophobia*. By the mid-nineties, each of their scores had surpassed the million mark.

———

Tonight, the stakes are high. If Mr. Evans is to die with even a modicum of self-respect, he must finally pull ahead. While Mrs. Evans clears the supper dishes, Mr. Evans sets up the game on the same teak table they've had since 1959. The last few Saturdays he has won. He is catching up.

To start, they each pull a card from the face-down deck. Mr. Evans gets the letter *b*, Mrs. Evans the letter *k*. A good sign. Every game has its element of luck and Mr. Evans is lucky. He will be the dealer. He will go first.

"I can die," he says. "I'm a hair's breadth away."

Mr. Evans is an aviation specialist, not a gambler, but just this morning, ruminating on the back porch, he had made his own bet. He hasn't told Mrs. Evans his numbers are skyrocketing or that the doctor gave him six months.

Nor has he told her that Macondo, the Chicago-based Pan-Asian transportation firm where he's become a senior partner, is currently in the crosshairs of the International Trade Administration, the Thailand Board of Investment, and the Association of Southeast Asian Nations, for its alleged role in what is fast becoming an Asian currency crisis.

"What did you say, Lenny?"

"I said I can die as soon as I get more points than you, dear."

Mr. Evans has spent the entire afternoon imagining this unlikely victory. Tonight, he will lie on his side of their king-size bed and Mrs. Evans, trounced for the first time, will be quiet, the room almost peaceful. His blood cells will be free to procreate like rabbits in his bone marrow.

Mrs. Evans is attractive even when she scowls. She doesn't know he's not joking. She looks at her fingernails, which she has polished with clear lacquer. Mr. Evans feels like a scoundrel, which feels good. Dying, it turns out, gives him an advantage. Perhaps he doesn't need to actually win the game. Perhaps, by this simple proposition, linking his death to his score, he has already won.

"That's absurd," she says, pushing a few short curls off her forehead. He feels it, too, even in shorts and open shirt, the heat left over from the day. Her face looks dour. He notices a slight crookedness in her once-starlet looks—Susan Hayward, he used to say; Elizabeth Taylor, she still insists. There is an unexpected softness in her jowl that moves him. On every shelf, tucked away in every niche, are the miniature ceramic pots Mrs. Evans has collected when Mr. Evans allows her to accompany him on business trips to Manila or Bangkok.

"You're not going to die, Lenny," she says with her signature wry smile, the one that usually defeats him.

Mr. Evans focuses on the fourteen cards laid out on the table, two horizontal rows, seven facing her and seven facing him. Each card has a big black letter on it and each letter is worth zero to four points. He can use any of these cards to make a word—as long as it can be found in the Oxford dictionary and starts with a letter in his row. He can also steal a word from Mrs. Evans. Her *lace*, for example, could be placed on his *p* just waiting there in his row.

Mr. Evans feels heady tonight, quickly seeing over a dozen

words he could make, all with decent scores. The fluffed-up Persian brushes his calf, turning her uppity behind in his direction, apparently desiring a rub. He pats her on the head. Her claws shoot out and she whacks at his leg, drawing two faint lines of blood.

"Do something," Mrs. Evans says, growing impatient. She gets up to retrieve the red plastic egg timer from the spice rack and turns it on its head. The white sand sifts down.

Mr. Evans puts a word on the table, a sweet word, a good word, *lethargy*, 64 points, not bad considering he had only two vowel cards to work with and is suffering from jet lag—he has only just returned from another business trip to Bangkok.

But seconds after he deals replacement cards for the ones he's just used, Mrs. Evans slaps down *sarcophagus*, 77 points, keeping her lead.

Mr. Evans's calf is still bleeding where the cat's claw cut deep. He studies the cards and sees the word *rent*, a lousy 12 points. He forages in his brain for a better choice, but encounters a recent memory of Vilai instead, still handsome in her forties, bent over her sewing machine in the Suriwong Sewing Shop he pays for. If only she were here, she would crouch on the carpet in her house slippers and apply Ya-Sa-Marn-Phlae with her expert hands, soothing him with her honeyed words, comforts he will miss.

He glances at Mrs. Evans to see if she has noticed his reverie, but her eyes are on the cards. She is toying with her wedding band, slipping it on and off, already calculating her next play.

Before she was Mrs. Evans, Mr. Evans brought his fraternity brothers with him to sing "The Sweetheart of Sigma Chi" to her below her second-story dorm window. He still wants to win her over.

Twenty-four years ago, flashy Mr. Matsuda, Mr. Evans's Japanese partner at Macondo—dubbed "Prince of Patpong" by the Americans due to his clout in Bangkok's red-light district—cajoled Mr. Evans into meeting Vilai, a young bargirl at the Cosmos Club. It was 1973, the year the Thai government purchased and drained Nong Ngu Hao, Cobra Swamp, so they could build a new airport and make Bangkok an international hub. The king of Thailand had named the proposed airport Suvarnabhumi, meaning realm of gold. Mr. Evans and Mr. Matsuda were Macondo's advisors on the project, which, once built, would have the tallest freestanding control tower in the world.

"The beautiful Vilai," Mr. Matsuda had said, bowing as she stepped out from the cluster of Chengmai girls with her sullen eyes and her silky yellow dress. She leaned in close as if she knew Mr. Evans, her gold bracelets jangling, her skin sallow under the neon lights. Bashful with women, Mr. Evans blushed. She was twenty-two, just a few years older than Mr. Evans's eldest.

Vilai slid her hand into his and let him lead her into the busy street. Outside in the dusk, two grinning boys came up for air after a dive from a rickety bridge into the *klong*, which smelled faintly of petroleum and rotting fish. After a sweltering day of sellers bargaining from their boats, the bitter-sweet scent of sun-drenched mangos and durian still lingered. In spare English, Vilai explained to Mr. Evans that it was Loy Krathong, the annual Thai full moon celebration in honor of the Mother of Water. "You are lucky man," she said. Hundreds of tiny floating baskets, each one shaped from a banana leaf and lit with a single candle, sailed up and down the klong. Mr. Evans laughed with uncustomary ease, but all at once Vilai stopped talking. The baskets had clustered along the klong's borders, some invisible current pushing them against its walls. They skittered like manic water bugs. One by one, their flames went out.

The top of the egg timer is empty. Mr. Evans begins to lay down *rental*, hesitantly, pausing on the *n*—the points are so low—to count the score and see if he hasn't missed something obvious that his wife sees. Her steel-blue eyes are intent on the letters. Her wavy black hair, barely a strand of gray, is cropped short in the back and layered stylishly around her face. He puts down the *t-a-l* and leans back in his chair with an air of triumph—false, he knows, even foolish.

"You take too long," Mrs. Evans says, snatching five cards from the top of the pile and placing them face up in the empty spaces.

"I'm the dealer," says Mr. Evans.

"Not anymore," she says.

The Evanses met in college on a scavenger hunt organized by her sorority for his fraternity—she in her plaid skirt, saddle shoes, and Susan Hayward do; he, sandy hair slicked back, straight out of naval officer school. They were a team. They knocked on doors and asked for eight clothespins, five rubber bands, a clean diaper, two golf balls, four bobby pins, and a slice of homemade pie. Together, they had won.

Mr. Evans gets up to dish chocolate ice cream into bowls. The ice cream is rock-hard but Mr. Evans is strong. He hopes Mrs. Evans notices. He can feel her eyes on him.

"Don't leave the freezer door open, Lenny," she says.

Mr. Evans recalls the large schools of carp that slipped through the water in front of the Royal Siam on his first visit to Bangkok, their neon orange darkening when a cloud passed the sun. The hotel employees, inordinately chipper behind their desks, annoyed him. Emblazoned on the red-carpet trail along the corridor, Thai lettering extolled the king. Mr. Evans's large Western shoes pressed into its weave as he looked for his room on the twenty-third floor, his jacket slung over his shoulder, perspiration spreading under his arms.

"The freezer, Lenny."

Bangkok's heat stripped him of every thought of Mrs. Evans seated in her classroom correcting long division in another hemisphere. In his hotel room, shirtless, he sat on the corner of the perfectly made bed and let gravity call him down onto the silken spread, still in his shoes. He could feel his heart move slowly inside his chest, aimlessly, like the fat carp in the lava pond.

Mrs. Evans treated Mr. Evans diplomatically when the doctor first told him about his preleukemia six years ago, bestowing on him a tenderness he'd forgotten she was capable of. On the shoulder or forehead, an unexpected kiss. You will get bruises, the doctor explained then. They will come and go. You could live a long time.

The Evanses decided to tell no one. Not even their children. Any bruises would be hidden beneath his clothes. But Mrs. Evans saw them, blue islands floating on her husband's skin. She drew a map showing eleven discolorations. As they disappeared, she crossed them out. After each blood test, she graphed the numbers. Meanwhile, she coddled him, even letting him win the game a few times by not stealing, for example, his word *front* to make *confront*. He knew she had seen it. But the years went by and he didn't die, though the feeling of uncertainty was there in Mr. Evans's stomach most of the time.

"You probably don't care what happened at school today," he hears Mrs. Evans say. Though she has added global education and astronomy to the curriculum, teaching reading, writing, and arithmetic to fourth graders for a quarter century has never completely satisfied her, a sentiment she frequently shares with him. She plans to retire at the end of the year. "I could solve every world problem," she likes to say, "if only the Secretary-General would ask me." She has taken over the ice cream scooping now, exactly two scoops each, as is their custom, and Mr. Evans has returned to the table. He tries to forget Vilai. He wants to be attentive to Mrs. Evans, to indulge her so she feels less competitive—she is smarter than him—and more likely to let her guard down in the game.

"It was just after recess. Not yet time for lunch," she says, sliding the ice cream container into the freezer. From the back, with her compact figure and shapely legs, Mrs. Evans could be in her twenties. She turns and faces Mr. Evans. "'Look at your shoes,' I told my kids. 'The oil used to make the soles came from Saudi Arabia.' I got my tallest student to pull down the map. I used my pointer to show them the huge pink shape abutting the Persian Gulf on the west and on the east, the Red Sea. 'Why do they call it red?' 'How come Sardi-rabia is pink?' 'Shush,' I said, 'that isn't the point.'"

Mrs. Evans sets the bowls on the table, the ice cream already melting. Completely involved now in her story, she leans forward, still standing, until she is tilting precariously over their Bali game. Mr. Evans puts his arms out as if to catch her. He enjoys her stories, which she often tells in odd places or in between things: at night when he is trying to go to sleep, in the car in the club parking lot when they are late for a bridge game, after the bill has come for dinner. Her enthusiasm comforts him. Her anecdotes, which are never boring, fill the emptiness.

"'Everyone put one foot up on your desk,' I said to my kids. You can imagine. Thirty-two clunks, shrieks of laughter. 'Good job,' I said. 'Where do you think the material used to make the top of your shoes comes from?' 'Japan,' everyone said. They were so certain. 'China?' someone wondered. 'Pakistan,' I said. 'And the laces are made from cotton grown in India. The shoes were assembled in Mexico. This is the point.' There was utter silence. No rolling pencils. No spitballs. All sixty-four eyes were on me. I could feel their brains expanding, Lenny, every one of them. Then I said the magic words that get me up at six every morning to slice that half a banana you always leave me onto my Raisin Bran and head to East Kankakee. 'Children,' I said, 'if you remember nothing else, please remember this: *we are all connected.*'"

Mr. Evans feels for the scratches on his leg. They are already beginning to scab. He knows exactly what Mrs. Evans is thinking. Doing her small part to stem what she calls "the tide of ignorance and national narcissism" has never been enough for her. Education is a game she can never win. But this doesn't stop her from trying. Mr. Evans admires her for this.

"Ideas become obsolete," she says, settling back down in her chair. "People lie." She examines their columns of cards, now covering half the table. "Letters and numbers, on the other hand, do not." She uses the wild card—one of two in the deck and worth five points—adding it, together with an *e*, to pluralize *sarcophagus*, increasing the word's score by 79 points.

Mr. Evans is leaning so far back in his chair it is balancing on two legs.

"You're going to fall, Lenny," Mrs. Evans says without looking up. Then she rests her chin on her hand and frowns like a child. She looks at Mr. Evans.

"Did you see her this time?" she asks, refusing to say Vilai's name.

Mr. Evans doesn't answer. Instead he pushes away what is left of his ice cream and gets up to pour himself a Scotch on the rocks. He had promised he wouldn't see Vilai. He always promises and Mrs. Evans always takes him back. One time, early on, he actually kept that promise, meeting with government officials without informing Vilai he was in Bangkok. But the Cosmos Club operated more like an extended family than a business, and she found out. It has never been easy for Mr. Evans to end things. His Nebraskan parents schooled him from birth to be polite.

"The flap of a moth in Bangkok," Mrs. Evans says.

"Makes thunder in Illinois," Mr. Evans says. "I know."

All those years ago, when the children were in junior high school, gonorrhea had tipped her off—surreptitious bottles of tetracycline, the itching and burning in her groin, the fevers she never let him forget.

"I'm sorry," he says.

The previous Saturday, he'd found Mrs. Evans in the garden inviting twilight birds to the bird feeder she'd hung ten years before in the dogwood. She called them by name, Vixen and Comet, as if they were reindeer. How does she tell them apart, he wondered, all brown sparrows? She always seems relaxed among her roses, laughing at his jokes, too engrossed in weeding and pruning to pay attention to his failings. He filled the garbage can with what she had trimmed without her asking. She pointed out the sunset, and he watched it with her.

"Will you go back?" she says now. It is difficult for Mr. Evans to look at her when she is about to cry. Her eyes tarnish like unpolished silver.

In the course of his work, he has left her alone for weeks and months at a time before returning in a handsome new suit, custom-made in Thailand, to their front door. But Mrs. Evans is not easily impressed. Nor does her rancor seem to wane in his absence. Rather than spend his evenings with her on their living room couch and dodge her slights, many well deserved, Mr. Evans prefers to play computer solitaire in his home office, usually losing, all the while yearning for a little unsolicited sweet talk from his wife. If she has been unwilling, he has been incapable of traversing that much separation.

So they play Bali.

Mrs. Evans lays her hand face up on the table as if she wants Mr. Evans to cover it with his.

"Of course, I'll go back," he answers her. "The realm of gold, remember?" He smiles, allowing himself a moment of swagger, knowing full well his position is in peril, the Thai *baht* capsizing as they speak.

Mrs. Evans, who has recently become the membership chair of the United Nations Association in Cook County, is not in the mood for humor.

"They need peace in Thailand, not airports," she says. "Not high-interest loans they can never pay back."

Mrs. Evans, who can't know the half of it, has asked him many times to cut ties with Macondo's "deceitful ways" and get a decent job in Bradley.

Mr. Evans looks past her, out the window where he sees an oriole fly onto the tiny roof of the bird feeder and scan the yard for threat. A throng of full-throated peonies seems to float against the weather-beaten fence. Beyond their splendid pink, the sea of corn spreads out endlessly like a veil ripped here and there by a tractor or pierced by a silo on fire, reflecting the sun.

Thailand's transition from military to civilian rule has not been easy. There have been nine constitutions and multiple, sometimes bloody, reversals along the way. Each time there has been a coup, Mr. Evans has had to switch loyalties for the sake of the airport project, while remaining in the good graces of the king. It is impossible for Mrs. Evans to imagine living with that level of uncertainty.

Mr. Matsuda, a one-time professional boxer, was the only person in the world Mr. Evans could talk to about anything other than business. "Why do you live like this, plunged in sorrows?" the Prince of Patpong asked him each year. In 1992, just before the horrors that would later be called Black May, Mr. Evans confided that Mrs. Evans had found Vilai's fragrance on his clothes for the umpteenth time and had finally kicked him out of the house.

"You always let yourself get carried along," Mrs. Evans had shouted, as she threw things into his bags. "When will you ever tack into the goddamn wind?"

Mr. Evans had bumped into the hanging lantern in the foyer as he exited the house, having forgotten to duck his head. There would soon be an unwarranted bruise there the size of a fist, a nasty symptom of preleukemia. He would have to buy a cap. He heard Mrs. Evans yelling behind him. His black bags lay strewn on the front stoop where she had flung them.

"Good morning," the congenial garbageman had said, jumping down from his truck to haul away their trash. "Heading to the expressway, Mr. Evans?" Mr. Evans managed a brisk smile and threw his bags—had he remembered the Don Mueang projections?—into the backseat of his VW bug. Behind him, the scrape of the metal garbage cans against the driveway alarmed him, as if confirming his new refugee status. He could get a motel room in Kankakee or Chicago, or he could fly to Bangkok.

He had pushed the driver's seat back, worked his long legs in, and rolled down the little window, which wasn't easy, its encasement sticky from years of humidity. For three decades he has forced his giant frame into this bug without air-conditioning in one-hundred-degree summer heat, hunched and fetal, the tiny, hard steering wheel pressing into his chest. They could afford a Lexus, but Mrs. Evans has refused to let him buy one until their 1967 twin convertible bugs, already collector's items, are worth five times their original price. Another one of her made-up games.

The old engine turned over fast. He wondered if Mrs. Evans would change her mind and come to their front door as she often did, to remind him to get some milk on the way home or tell him his collar was sticking up. The custom was irritating, and yet its absence would be unpleasant.

Mrs. Evans did come out, her eyes red-rimmed, her fists held like a doll's at her sides.

"Don't come back!" she yelled.

Then the front door to his home had slammed shut.

Mrs. Evans, who has won the first game of the evening, is reshuffling for another round. Mr. Evans pours himself another Scotch. He hadn't checked into a local hotel that time. He had driven to O'Hare and flown to Bangkok.

When he arrived at the Cosmos, everyone was drunk. They were always drunk, ordering more beers, the *farang*, white men in business suits, with one or two Thai women sitting decorously on their laps. Mr. Matsuda, surprised to see him, toasted Mr. Evans in front of the crowd as if he had achieved something important.

"A free man," Mr. Matsuda announced. "A great American man."

But leaving Mrs. Evans had not been his choice. And the Suvarnabhumi project was failing miserably. Not one ceremonial stone had been laid down at Cobra Swamp by king or contractor in all these years. But that hadn't stopped Macondo from its latest development scheme. Foreign capital was finally pouring in.

Outside the bar, throngs of people had surged into the town square: fruit vendors, lottery vendors, noodle vendors, prostitutes, Bangkok's youth, all decrying General K, who was in bed with foreign businessmen, who were, like Mr. Matsuda, in bed with the king, though no one dared accuse the king directly. Monks were there, too, marching in the humid streets in their saffron robes, their dark, bald heads forming a long line of protest. Tuk tuks parked, cluttering the roads. Samlors silenced their bells. In just three days, fifty-three people, chanting and wearing yellow arm bands, many of them university students, had been killed by Thai soldiers. Thousands more had been injured, arrested and tortured, or disappeared.

Mr. Evans sipped his cocktail without heart, while at his side, Vilai held forth about Thailand's "wreck of a democracy" with the animated Thai men and women at their table. The group went silent when the king, dressed in his customary white suit braided with gold, appeared on the small TV screen behind the bar. Across from His Majesty, sitting so close they looked like a couple, were General K, leader of the most recent coup, and General C, leader of the opposition. Meanwhile, gunshots rang outside. "Eventually," the king said to his people, "the People don't know why they're fighting each other. They just know they have to win." He paused. Vilai was doing her best to translate. "But to what purpose," the king said, "are you telling yourself that you're the winner when you're standing upon ruins?"

Mr. Evans wanted to go back to his hotel and write a postcard to Mrs. Evans: not his usual witty anecdotes about airplane meals in business class and the headache of lost luggage, but the ways his firm has been complicit in Thailand's fickle networks of corruption, things he's been strictly forbidden to tell her.

He wanted to write "I love you" in his tiny print. At home the words always caught in his throat. But after another round of drinks, Mr. Matsuda got him to sing. They all cried out for it: *Leonard Evans, Leonard Evans,* they called, all of which flustered him, tone-deaf as he was, something Mrs. Evans reminded him each Christmas Eve as he sang, without restraint, "Hark! The Herald Angels Sing." Which is what he sang now at the Cosmos, everyone laughing, trying to sing along, even Vilai.

At four a.m., Mr. Matsuda's driver chauffeured the two men from the Cosmos to Mr. Evans's hotel, the streets finally quiet. Vilai sat between them, a little giddy, even clumsy in her designer swath of silk. As soon as Mr. Matsuda left the hotel room, she unfurled the scarves she wore over her blouse and watched him, her third farang of the day, awkwardly disengage his belt. Vilai's refusal to give up her transactions was something Mr. Evans, having granted her what he considered to be a decent means of living, took pains not to think about.

A muted honking outside the window seemed to turn in on itself. Vilai put her familiar hands on Mr. Evans's broad shoulders, and gasped, his bruises shocking her with their gem-like blue. She prodded him gently down and slipped off her dress. A gifted storyteller, that night she did not speak. Through the years, Mr. Evans had come to rely on the sangfroid of her confidence.

Mr. Evans glances at Mrs. Evans, pushes his chair back, and gets up from the table Mrs. Evans insists he refinish every three years. He wants to play Chet Baker, whose voice, sexier than a sax, says everything Mr. Evans has never dared to say. His wife is concentrating on the letters. In the cabinet are all the records, the ones they bought together; the ones he bought alone to savor after his daily commute from Chicago, lying on the couch or in the chair swing on the porch at dusk; the ones the children danced to in the living room when they were young. Mr. Evans lays the record on the turntable and places the needle on its outer edge. Chet Baker croons. Mr. Evans swoons, outside now on the porch, swaying beneath the dappled sky.

"I can't think," Mrs. Evans says, "with all that noise." She doesn't look up. She has taken a couple of cards from his row and is holding them over hers, not quite ready to place them down on the table, calculating points in her head. She is losing.

Last summer, Mr. and Mrs. Evans visited their eldest daughter in California. On the second day, they left her reading Beckett in a bikini on the roof of her rent-controlled apartment and drove north to the Russian River. On its bank, Mr. Evans, who has a sixth sense for Bangkok time, rested his head on his wife's lap, shaded his eyes from the sun and thought about Vilai. She would, in that moment, be lying diagonally on her monsoon bed beneath her lacy mosquito net, a sarong draped across her breasts, calculating her savings or dreaming, breathing in the scent of dragon fruit and oil, lemongrass and dust. In his mind, he heard the rickshaw wheels creaking against the street, the honking of overstuffed commercial trucks reverberating against the thin walls of her apartment. In a harsh and competitive field, Vilai had told him, she was one of the most skilled at the game she played, a game of hazard and good luck. She knew how to seduce, how to decline, who to trust. Without her cleverness, she might not have survived. She could not count solely, she often reminded him, on his good will.

A cadre of ducks flew overhead, migrating south along the Russian River. But Mr. Evans's eyes were closed. He felt Vilai's practiced hands tracing the bruises on his legs and back, the texts by which she had come to know him, then stroking his shoulders, deliberate and constant like the paddles of market vendors dipping and pulling through the klong's dark waters.

"You're frowning," Mrs. Evans told him as she pushed at the furrows on his forehead, forcing them smooth.

Back in his living room, Mr. Evans dances to Chet as the room darkens, colliding with the rocking chair in his exuberance. It rocks then rights itself. He dances toward his wife, stretching out his hand. The sky is purple. She seizes on a word.

"Hexagonal," she says. It is amazing. How does she do it? She is wearing a sleeveless blouse and her freckled arms look delicious in the afterglow of sunset. She rests her forefinger on the 90-point word that puts her in the lead and smiles up at him. *But I fall in love too easily, I fall in love too fast,* Chet sings before discharging his melancholy through his trumpet.

Mr. Evans is not thinking now of revenge or death.

"Please," he says, standing in front of his wife like his mother taught him to do. "May I have this dance?" Mrs. Evans leans back in her chair and switches on the light. He clicks it off just as the streetlight comes on beyond the driveway and he lifts her from the old teak chair, lifts her to her feet and gathers her in his arms. She is so small and light on her feet, even now. She lays her head against his chest and they turn in the dark.

Later, Mr. Evans is drunk—the Rutherford from supper, the

Johnnie Walker Black—and they are still playing game two. It's 1,232,957 to 1,232,896. Mr. Evans has rallied.

He feels bruises in places nothing has touched, coming up to the surface like stains. *Taxonomy.* He sees it but can't believe it. He uses his *x* and her lips are soft and set. He can't remember when she first said he was the cause of her loneliness. He holds tight to the blame. He doesn't mean to, but at night when he and Mrs. Evans turn on the fan and lie back against the coolness of the sheet on separate sides of their king-size bed, he often feels it in his blood and smells its rotten scent.

Mr. and Mrs. Evans usually play one or two games at most on a single evening. But tonight Mr. Evans insists on a third, determined to win again. It's midnight, Mrs. Evans's witching hour, when her armor comes off and she hangs her javelins at the door. She looks worried and she should be. She is close to losing her lifetime lead. She asks if they can play this last game on the back porch in candlelight. There will be a meteor shower tonight.

Outside, the air is warm and faintly sweet with the scent of corn pollen. Mr. Evans watches Mrs. Evans pull the cards from their box, shuffle them expertly, and deal him seven cards face up in a line, then seven for herself. She looks beautiful in the semi-dark. Perhaps overconfident, Mr. Evans lets her go first but immediately regrets it when she quickly puts down *difficulties*, two *f*'s, three *i*'s, a miracle, using almost all the letters on the table. Above them meteors crash and burn in broad arcs from different quadrants of the sky. Mrs. Evans is counting them. Three. Eight. Thirteen. Her game is to see twenty falling stars.

"Lenny! Fifteen!" She reaches for his hand, but he is concentrating on the game, carefully selecting letters from her column.

"Yep," he says. "They're falling."

He wracks his brain for polysyllabic words. There are no high-point letters on the table. The moon appears over the fence. Mrs. Evans doesn't rush him.

He suddenly sees it. He can use his word *ðen* and the *sch* he'd put down hoping for *schism* or *schema*. He lays down his cards.

"That's a foreign word," Mrs. Evans says. "You're not allowed to use foreign words."

Mr. Evans jumps up and jogs inside to get the dictionary, hitting the transom of the sliding door with his head.

"Crap," he says.

But there it is plain as day in the dictionary. *Schaðenfreuðe*. 118 points.

When he returns, Mrs. Evans comes to his side of the table and surprises him by sitting on his lap as if the more he closes the gap between their scores, the more she adores him for his pluck. "Sixteen," she calls out, looking up at the sky. Then she steals his *easy* to make *queasy*. With Mrs. Evans sitting sidesaddle, the two of them come up with word after word until there are only two cards left to draw from. Mrs. Evans deals the wild card.

Mr. Evans uses it now as a *y* to make *zephyr* and wins the game, surpassing his wife's cumulative points for the first time in their marriage.

He has won his own secret bet, which frightens him. There is nothing more he has to do.

"Congratulations!" Mrs. Evans says, without irony, hardly the reaction he would expect. She invites him to join her on their twin chaise lounges beneath the stars. He pulls his close to hers and they lie next to each other on their backs.

Mr. Evans, of course, *did* see Vilai again this last time.

She sent her three employees out and lay down next to him. The Suriwong Sewing Shop had a Closed sign in the window for the one hour she gave him. Her brother was sick like a dog, she told him, rubbing his bruises so indelicately he asked her to stop. As a favor, could he give her money for the hospital bill? "You will die soon," she said. "You might not come back."

When Mr. Evans agreed to pay, she unwrapped her sarong, then told a joke as he unbuttoned his shirt. But it wasn't funny. "You're not *farang* anymore," she said. Meaning white. "You're *si ka*." Meaning dark blue.

He doesn't tell Mrs. Evans his liaison with Vilai is over.

Out on the back porch, the axis of the earth seems to shift. Mr. Evans can feel it, but he doesn't understand it. Is it the sudden scent of dogwood flung toward him on the late-night breeze? Or perhaps Mrs. Evans's exclamation: the nineteenth star? She dishes new bowls of ice cream, two scoops each, and brings them out to the porch. Next Saturday, they will play the game again. She is certain she will pull ahead. "I won't let you die, Lenny," she tells him as she gathers the cards from the table, hitting them softly against its surface, dividing them into two decks and fitting them neatly side by side.

CITY OF ANGELS

We wanted to be ravished. The Jewish girls leaving their nouveau riche houses on the east side of Overland Avenue, the Catholic girls released from their meager tract homes on the west. We were the popular girls and the wannabes. Every Saturday morning, we piled onto the Pico #7 bus at the corners of Beverwil and Manning, where we met the opposite sex—pop, nerd, and dweeb—and rode west, a ride without parents, heaven waiting at the end of the line.

I was a wannabe, a flat, skinny Protestant-Jewish mongrel, a girl without prospects, attached at the hip to my best friend, a beauty with full Sephardic lips and black hair. Yet those Saturdays felt like my heaven, too, as the big bus roared in us, opening the throttle to last weekend's spin the bottle in someone's cold basement, our skimpy Liz Claiborne beachwear smelling like new blue-crystal Tide. We were a busload of angels, buoyant in the glare, the Southern California sun blasting our windows.

"Did you see the size of his thing?" my best friend whispered in my ear, referring to the burly bus driver in dazzle mirror shades with his foot on the thrust lever, the man who ferried us every weekend to the Promised Land. I hadn't noticed. "Amazing!" I whispered back as we pushed our way through the crowded aisle to the screaming back of the bus and scooched thigh to thigh onto the hot vinyl seat. I inhaled her Aqua Net. I savored the sweet citrus on her breath. She who, after years of hopscotch and sleepovers, harmonizing Girl Scout camp songs, and cracking up over tuna salad on Ritz, so suddenly had the uncanny ability to detect penile attributes within the folds of baggy pants on any boy or man and from any distance. Since third grade, we'd spent every spare minute swapping jokes, tears, and confidences.

"Hey, Susie, Joyce!" she said twisting around to the popular girls and blowing them kisses. It was the summer of 1965. I was losing her.

The Promised Land was Santa Monica Beach, wide as the Mississippi, a place where algebra equations and seventh-grade report cards dissolved along with all recollection of metal lockers banging between periods or cavernous hallways the color of stale chocolate. We disembarked in chatty clusters, lured by the Pacific's blaze of heat and salt air and headed to Station 8, where the nerds and dweebs respectfully fanned out and disappeared, leaving us the prime real estate. Here, below the lifeguard station, the lanky, brown-haired boys spread their bold beach towels gently on the sand, jangling their silver ID bracelets, a kind of mating call, their junior high school rings glinting carmine, prospecting for love.

A few feet away, the popular girls laid down their unmolested bodies, a menagerie of nubile breasts lurking in their falsie triple-A bikini cups, or, for the chosen few, plump as casaba melons. The popular boys, now naked to the waist, longed to touch just one with newly bar mitzvahed hand or tongue. Meanwhile, the girls swooned in their own eighteen-karat flotsam—crucifixes and Stars of David hanging from their necks. The lone gentile boy, a blond surfer, proffered his coveted Saint Christopher on his sunbaked chest. By the end of the day, it would surely be dangling in some frisky girl's cleavage.

At Station 8, popularity had no religion. Where you laid your beach towel in the sand signaled whether you were in or out. I laid mine on the outer edge. My best friend, newly bosomed, a magnet for all the bitchin' boys, joined the popular girls in the inner ring. What remained: our separate bodies and our ache. I ached for her. She ached for him, the son of a kosher butcher. Our friendship vanished that day in the quixotic light.

But I could see her. I did not fan out. I was not a popular girl, but I was not a dweeb either. I did what the popular girls did. We laid ourselves carefully on our backs, our legs shining from the obligatory early morning shave, our armpits as pink and clean as seashells. Slowly, we crooked our heads so we could see how we looked, admiring our harp-shaped ribs descending into the soft platter of the belly, then down to the narrow horizon of our hips.

Here at Station 8 we had no protection. Our beach towels strained to hold us in, free from the threat of sand or tiny shore flies blemishing our flawless skin. Strained to hold our big purses with all their white lip gloss and the Laura Scudder's barbecue potato chips, Giant Size, and the Doublemint gum and transistor radio with extra batteries and the tease comb and the neon plastic brush from Drug King and the hairspray to keep the frozen-juice-can curls in place and *Wuthering Heights*, fleecy with rereading—oh, how we swooned for Laurence Olivier's Heathcliff—and a wallet with clear plastic sheaths to hold the yearbook photo of our boyfriend and our best friends and our past boyfriends and their bitchin' older brothers with enough coins to pay for the bus ride home, one chocolate-dipped vanilla cone, and two small pink lemonades.

Here on the beach, blood was just beginning to run. Two out of three of us were cramping. Those using Tampax surreptitiously probed their inner thighs, hoping not to encounter the wayward string, praying the cotton tampon would not be lost forever inside them. Those wearing Kotex flattened the noxious bulge with their palms and repeatedly checked for leaking. The ones with pubic hair suddenly scrambling out of their bikini crotches were advised about waxing.

Everyone cared about hair. The ones who slept on cans to straighten their curls took out their plastic hand mirrors to puff up their perfectly haloed heads while the straight-haired girls who went to bed with tight pink sponge curlers around their necks took out their plastic brushes to fluff up their do-or-die gravity-defying symmetrical flips. Meanwhile, the boys, silky with peach fuzz and coiffed like Elvis, wondered if their allowance would cover an electric Remington and when they would need one.

By noon the air was clear to Catalina. The Fosters Freeze and hot dogs on a stick from the nearest beach stand perfumed the stagnant weight of summer. A few gulls scavenged the blue air for its sweet smell. But I was also there, locked into the gravitational pull of Station 8, alone and in heat. Though my blood did not yet run and my flip had gone limp. Though I didn't really want a boy. I listened to the gulls' episodic cries overlaid with the Beach Boys' *Help me, Rhonda; help, help me, Rhonda*, its tinny vibrato playing through a dozen spoon-sized speakers, a vibration that settled in the sweat that never caught in my cleavage because there was no cleavage.

Wanna go steady? the son of a butcher said, his voice a jumble of soprano and baritone. I shifted to my side to see him on his knees, his smooth triangular back angling toward my best friend. Her eyelids fluttered, I swear they did, like Natalie Wood's. *Yes*, she said, *yes*, and slipped on his bracelet. Fait accompli. He now owned her.

I turned to see the muscular Station 8 lifeguard high up on his throne of peeling red paint, tanned beyond recognition, his binoculars seeming to scan the horizon for drowning children. But I knew what he was looking at. Like a cliff hawk, he watched the popular girls turn from back to front to bake, pulling off bikini straps to elude the enemy suntan line on their smooth shoulders, licking their hot lips, his wet dreams. He was older, out of high school. He didn't see me. His eyes passed over scrawny field mice and rested furtively on my best friend. Together, we watched her, Diana Ross throaty now on the radio: *I've got this burnin', burnin', yearnin' feeling inside me*, the other girls singing along. My heart could barely hold me in.

No one deigned look at the ocean, its unrepentant tide

repeating a message we were unable to hear above Mick Jagger's pouty crooning. No way. We were in LA. On the edge. Gambling for a smattering of attention and sun lotion from the palms of a young man's hands. Can you do my back, Rachel? Start with a girl. Show them how we touch. The way our quick piano-playing fingers press into the nape of the neck and work the cool white balm into the skin down both sides of the spine opening over the budding fullness of the hips. We invited them to our towels without inviting them to our towels. We were chirpy, raw diamonds in the sand, showing off recent orthodontry. Nothing else existed beyond our prime patch of beach.

But what were we aiming at, our vaginal lips wet with sweat, packed down into spandex triangles printed with tiny daisies, everything hidden and made-up? Something we'd glimpsed, perhaps, while touching ourselves at dawn beneath floral sheets, or accidentally grazing the full roundness of a girlfriend's new breast on the way to French—fueled by an insatiable desire to be seized and transported to another realm; to feel, in every cell, the ecstasy our hormones promised us. Yet something more mystical than that, something beyond our lust and yearning, beyond our hymns and mitzvahs, something we couldn't possibly imagine, lathering each other on our towels under the brassy Southern California sky.

———

Years later, on a business trip to LA, I ran into my old best friend. I'd fallen for a woman by then. And had C-cup breasts.

She'd been in and out of love with a poker hand of boyfriends. Now she lived alone. *I missed you*, she said. We sat on the sunny patio of a café in Venice Beach. I held her hand across the table while she wept. *My skin burns as if my body were on fire*, she told me. *I take Xanax and trazodone to survive. I can't sleep.* I knew just how she felt. Our innocence, we'd been unable to protect. She leaned toward me, tilting her head to the side like a rueful child. My childhood familiar. I could have lived inside those eyes. But I directed her gaze toward the beach. I didn't yet reveal my own punishments: bulimic in high school, sexually assaulted in college, raped by a stranger at gunpoint at twenty-four. I didn't want to worry her. Instead, I reminded her about those Saturdays in the sun when we were almost thirteen; when we wanted to be wanted so much we preened for hours; when, licking the vanilla swirls in blond sugar cones and waiting for the salt air and sunlight to open up our skin, we thought ravishment meant rapture.

OVERTURE

Mark and the kids are in the living room as I lift the steak from the broiler and prick it, testing for blood. Mark likes it medium rare. Just home from work, he's doing his carousel pony routine, circling around the couch and bee-boo-bopping a zingy calliope tune with four-year-old Norma on his back in her frilly daffodil dress. He fakes a stumble, then makes a show of saving her from the fall, which cracks up the kids. I laugh, too, as I set dinner on the table. Mark gives me a wink. "Me too," Stevie calls out to Mark. Up goes ten-year-old Stevie.

At the kitchen table, Mark's hair is ruffled from the horse-play. Norma and Stevie sit at their places, shiny and breathless. Norma is ours; Stevie, mine, belongs to the heartbreaker who skipped town before he was born.

"Don't forget my school concert's tomorrow," Stevie says. The concert is the fifth graders' big event before graduation. They've been practicing all year. He knows how much I want to go.

"You'll do great," I say. I kiss him on the cheek.

"Are you coming?" he dares to ask.

Mark interrupts with his own plea for attention.

"Clinched three sales today," he says.

This after a string of rejections, knocking on doors. I'm proud of Mark. It isn't easy to sell a product that has no value until the buyer is dead. It's not like selling a spiffy car they can drive away in—something he reminds me of every time his commissions tank.

"I put the extra money down on an Appaloosa stallion," Mark says, pouring cold beer into his glass. Everyone but Norma knows this isn't true. Mark cuts into his meat. He says something about pirate's gold for our nest egg. He chews. Something about the steak.

"What, honey?" I ask, the *honey* because it comforts him.

Mark's jaw beats like a heart.

"You're not listening to me," he says.

"I *am* listening," I say. And, in fact, I always listen to him. I can't afford to miss a shift in pitch.

The kids stop their bickering.

Mark holds up his steak with a fork. Blood drips onto his plate.

"Too rare?" I ask, neutral like a nurse. "Too cooked?"

The kids' eyes land on me. The curtains are closed. They're always closed. Our small house is on a quiet street of small houses. *A cave dug from ancient limestone* is what precocious Stevie called it in third grade, his Stone Age year. In the fourth grade, he rattled on about the hard, greedy men of the Bronze Age. Now, a year later, all he talks about is the Iron Age. The weapons are strong, he says, and the people are miserable.

"I'll cook you another one," I say to Mark, getting up.

Mark skids his chair back and grabs my arm.

"Not in front of the kids," I beg.

He escorts me down the narrow hallway to our bedroom. The bed is made. Everything is neat because I have made it neat. Mark's cologne bottles are arranged in bowling pin formation on the dresser. Red dice are stacked in columns in a polished brass bowl. A glossy photo of a younger Mark and his mother, Ramona, is tilted just so in its black velvet frame.

I stand still and wait. Mark likes me to wait, calm, as if I want it. I concentrate on a spot on the wall where the blue paint's chipped from Mark's boot. I pretend it's the back door to La Scala in Milan. I try to guide my mind into it. It doesn't always work.

Mark's pupils jitter and spark. He hesitates. Then puts me in a choke with his pale, stubby hands. He's been trying hard not to hit my face. Last summer, a neighbor saw welts.

In the dresser mirror, I see him smack the woman I've become, a waif in gray fleece, broken tooth, blonde roots leaking into my Maria Callas hair, black as pitch. It's as if the first slap wakes up a hundred slaps just waiting in his hand.

I don't resist.

With each blow, I enter deeper into the chipped spot on the wall until I hear the opera house audience fussing with their programs. Mark throws my body against the dresser. But I'm not me anymore. I'm the Druid High Priestess Norma, taking center stage in my long white dress. I stand strong, facing Pollione, the handsome Roman commander of our occupiers who

I secretly love and with whom I've borne two children. In my head, I sing a perfect legato like I did in high school. *Oh! Di qual sei tu vittima.* My voice reverberates up to the grand chandelier and into the six gold-leafed tiers. I hold everything in. Mark wavers. He hates that I don't react. In song, I rage. Pollione has betrayed me. He's fallen in love with my closest friend, the young priestess Adalgisa. I refuse to weep. The audience erupts.

I wake on the bedroom floor. On the other side of the drapes, rain slaps the window. The night presses in. Mark is asleep on our bed. I limp to the bedroom next door. Norma and Stevie are asleep in their clothes. Stevie's flute case leans against the wall by his bed like a weapon he might need to fight off dream demons. The air is cool. I tuck their bedspreads around them, the ones they fought over last year when Mark bought them. Norma, who won the coin flip, got the spread with mitts and bats. Stevie got the hockey pucks. My snared angels. If there is a world out there, it has stopped.

Mark stumbles into the hall and ushers me to bed. He's sorry, he croons, his lips on my ear. I treasure his remorse. It's worth more than it costs. Sleep finally comes. But it doesn't last. I hear him get up. Even in the dark, I recognize the shame in the slack curve of his back. He stops at the dresser, opens a drawer. His midnight roulette. Will he reach for the Kleenex? Or the gun in his lockbox? My body goes numb beneath the comforter.

Walk eight miles a day, said the prison priest after Mark's first arrest. *Play hymns on your headset.* A therapist said, *Drive to the foothills and yell. Throw a hundred stones.* Mark did everything he was told. He pitched for his old baseball team on weekends. He joined a men's group. Nothing worked. He says he can handle it himself. But none of us can predict when the spring-loaded trap in his chest will snap down on his heart.

He returns to me, a silhouette. Tonight, it's Kleenex. His tears moisten my skin. With his ring finger, he traces my lips.

"Please don't," I say.

I hurt. I don't want to be touched. But Mark knows me like he knows his own body. He touches me in the hidden places where I like to be touched, soft, the way I like to be touched.

Stevie was four when Mark and I met. I was twenty-two, Mark twenty-six. First thing he did was bring us to Land Park to ride the carousel. Mark's crazy about horses. He bragged about the acre he said he'd bought up in the Lodi hills where he plans to stable real Appaloosas and dress them just like these painted ones.

Mark had big dreams and a life insurance license—the only trainee in San Joaquin County, he said, who hadn't quit—and a little house I could live in without blame or quarrels with my jilted mother, who doted on Mark from the moment they met. *Here's a guy can take care of you,* she said. *Let him.* She had her own boyfriends to deal with by then and was sick of being stuck at home with Stevie while I sold CDs at a counter to pay my share of the rent.

That day at the park, Mark asked me what *I* dreamed of. I told him I wanted to sing bel canto like Maria Callas.

"Mary who?" he asked.

"The famous opera singer," I told him.

I'd been one of the lucky ones. The Stockton Opera Guild handpicked me from choir my junior year to play the cigarette girl in *Carmen*, then Papagena in *The Magic Flute*. I told Mark how good it felt to be vaulted from boredom to stardom and sing to the rafters, then bow with my troupe to a room full of strangers. How taken I was by the drama in each story—men and women willing to lie and die for love. How I'd sung their songs loud in my head on the bus and at breakfast to drown out the rest.

Senior year, I ached for the prima donna role in Bellini's *Norma*. I failed chemistry that year, but I learned the entire Italian libretto. My voice coach taught me trills and arpeggios. I spent my evenings trying to widen the space between my mouth and my throat. I got the part.

Mark slapped me a high five. "You've got that go-get-'em gene that's hard to come by," he said.

"But I lost the lead role," I told him, "when I got pregnant with Stevie." For weeks, I'd managed to keep my secret, rehearsing in shapeless gowns I found in the costume room. But my body got too big to hide. The guild pulled me from the show.

Mark put his pitching arm around me and held me for the first time.

"You've got your voice, Margie," he said. "No one can take *that* away."

That got to me. Right there and then, I took a deep breath and attempted the first few bars of "Casta Diva." High Priestess

Norma pleas for peace to the Moon Goddess. *The time is not ripe for our revenge*, she sings to the ragged crowd of Druid worshippers who have no idea she's borne two children with the same man they plan to kill.

People in the park stopped, ice cream melting onto their hands as they listened. My voice soared and brimmed, then cracked and broke. That voice I loved, so out of practice.

"It'll come back," Mark said.

He fit Stevie in front of him on a rearing stallion and held him tight. I jumped up from the bench and waved each time they came into view. When the Wurlitzer stopped, I mounted the mare next to them and we made a pledge. Mark would get his horse and I'd get my bel canto. "What about me?" Stevie asked. "You get a daddy," I said.

But there were things Mark wanted that he didn't know he wanted, things I didn't know I had to give.

"Milk for my little kitten?" Mark says to Norma.

Today is a new day. Mark pours a glass for Norma, then one for Stevie. The light sneaks into the kitchen through a crack in the curtain, hard and golden. Stevie wears the Jordans Mark got him for his birthday and carries his little black flute case. Next year, Norma will go to kindergarten. Mark burns the toast. The rest of us lift our heads like dogs, sniffing for the wind shift.

Stevie breaks the silence. He tries again.

"My concert is tonight," he says, casual like he's asking for the salt. But I can tell he's desperate. This is his last chance.

"I could win the music camp scholarship."

The last time I came to a school event, he was in third grade.

"Mom?" he says. I elbow him. He knows better. I'm not allowed to leave the house. "I want you to come hear me play," he says. "I want you to be there for my solo."

The refrigerator hums, then stops. Mark turns from the toaster.

Stevie sits up in his chair like the little man he was when he faced the police. His face is flushed. He holds his fork tight in his fist.

"We're going to perform Morton Gould's 'American Salute,'" he announces for Mark's benefit. "And Bellini's 'Overture to *Norma*,'" he says for mine. I already know, of course. I've heard the familiar melody nightly through his bedroom door. Some evenings, I've sat on Norma's bed and watched him open his black case, assemble his flute, and play the simple, heart-wrenching grammar-school version of the overture. He glances at his sister.

"To Norma?" Norma asks, as if on cue. "That's funny," she says.

But Stevie prods her with his fork. I can see they've rehearsed it.

"Wow," Norma says, too loud. She scrambles out of her chair and over to her father.

"A song for my kitten?" Mark says to her. "Now that *is* something special." He kisses the top of her head and starts over with the toast, whistling "The Star-Spangled Banner," the one tune he knows by heart.

We each get a little cup of red juice and a plate with toast cut in a diagonal. There are scrambled eggs on top. I am still in my pajamas, long-sleeved to cover the bruises. Norma's hair looks gummy. She smells like talc.

"Mom?" Stevie says again. I know how eager he is to see me at the bake sale table with the PTA moms. He wants to be proud of me in public like he's proud of Mark. Mark plans the spring carnival at Stevie's school like his father did when he was a boy. He pals around with the principal, a starry-eyed guy who played first base on Mark's high school baseball team. The two of them hang out in bars, Mark's told me, sometimes goading each other until they're drunk, then coaxing all the customers to raise their shots for a toast: *Here's to first-rate schools for every child in America!*

"I want to go tonight," I say to Mark. A strategy I rarely use now. The truth.

Mark is holding the frying pan. He sets it back on the stove.

We are marble statues at the table, waiting for what he might do.

"Let's all go," he says—like it was his idea.

Stevie can't believe it. He starts jabbering about his "magic flute," how you have to have your mouth just the right shape, the shape for spitting rice, to draw out its sound. How flutes go back 43,000 years. "They're older than every other musical instrument," he says, "except the human voice." He looks at me.

Yes, I think, the one gift God gave me.

Mark grazes my cheek as I'm taking the chicken out to thaw, on his finger the same ring that marks me.

"I'll call you, babe," he says, forgetting that just last week he swatted my cell phone, my last link to the world, from my hand when I tried, like a fool, to call his mother—just to say hello—and ground it under his shoe like a lit cigarette.

Then he remembers. Something happens in his eyes, the way butter congeals on our uneaten toast.

But Mark restrains himself. I see how hard he's trying. I smile, then erase it, unsure what's best. He's good-looking in his insurance salesman suit: pinstriped shirt, paisley vest, brown slacks. He gives love pats to the kids' heads so fast they don't have time to duck, and one on my ass before walking out the door.

"Us, Mom?" Norma looks up at me, her pigtails uneven. "To Stevie's school?"

"That's what your father said," I say. I can still smell him, lime aftershave and the menthol scent of Angel Ice.

I'm not Mark's favorite woman. That honor would go to his mother, Ramona, a short, thick woman who wears blouses and pants in loud colors, chartreuse or pink, always with a matching scarf at her neck, and dyes her hair four times a year to match the seasons. The two of them play pool in the clubroom at Ramona's apartment complex in Oakdale when he visits, or spend the day shopping. Mark buys her things: a faux-leather recliner, a big-screen TV, a two-door refrigerator, which she hardly needs—she lives alone. When Mark tells one of his bawdy jokes, no one laughs harder than Ramona.

I used to look forward to our monthly visits, out on the open highway, sugar pine lining the Sierra foothills, all evidence hidden beneath clothes and makeup. Ramona seemed to enjoy digging out old photos of Mark. She showed off his diplomas, his baseball trophies, and his plastic horse collection—Shetlands, Appaloosas, and Kiger mustangs, which filled two entire walls, all the while observing me warily with her lazy eye. I sometimes wondered if she was scared I'd tell her what her only child was doing to me. I knew she knew. It doesn't take a genius.

I never asked Ramona questions. That was one of Mark's rules. But once, when Norma and Stevie were with Mark in the TV room, I asked her why Mark was so crazy about horses.

"His daddy used to ride for sport," she said. "When Mark was a toddler, he took him to ride the carousel each Sunday, then to Greenbriar Stables once he was grown. The two of them would ride for hours up there in the foothills. Once they rode all the way to Lodi." She smiled, remembering, and leaned toward me. "He loved his daddy," she confided, adjusting her neck scarf, "loved him more than me." She surprised me, then, by putting her hand on mine. I could tell she wanted an honest-to-God daughter-in-law. But she had rules, too. At the sound of Mark in the hallway, she drew back her hand.

"Norma, dear," she called. "Come play with your grandma."

I knew then Ramona would never be on my side. Mark was all she had.

Yet an unspoken trust somehow grew between us, something I didn't understand until my final visit last year.

Ramona and I were sitting kitty-corner in her bright kitchen while Norma and Stevie watched cartoons and Mark mowed the front lawn. Ramona's hair was dyed pale apricot.

Through the kitchen window, we watched Mark rake the cut grass into small piles. He saw us there and gave us a thumbs-up before dumping it into a bin.

"Mark's a good father," she said.

"Yes," I said, "he is."

"He makes good steady money."

"Yes, he does." She sounded like my mother.

Then she got up and started to sponge off the kitchen counter. She didn't hide her limp that day and when she turned to me, her broad, good-natured face looked crushed, sadder than I'd ever seen it. She took off her neck scarf and showed me the scar. A bullet or a knife, I couldn't tell.

"The man Mark is got decided before he ever had a chance to choose," she said. "What happened to me had nothing to do with him. I've told him a thousand times. But he can't seem to get it into his head."

I wondered why, now, she was confiding in me.

"To be honest, Margie," she said, "I can't tell you which one of the three of us deserves more pity in the eyes of God."

"*I* can," I said, my voice rising. "Only one of us is in any goddamn danger."

Now Mark doesn't take me anymore. But it was Ramona who had started the forbidden conversation.

———

Norma and I hear Mark's car pull away. It's exactly eight thirty. Mark's schedule is precise. Stevie makes sure he has his homework binder. I bend to zip his backpack and Norma traces my cheek as if touch could erase the swelling. She frowns. She is not the inheritor of hope.

"You're coming tonight," Stevie says. An order. But also a warning. I start to suspect it was his idea—coaxing the music teacher to attempt the "Overture to *Norma*" with fifth graders.

Once, when he was eight, he called the police. The two cops stood at our door, buttons gleaming, like a fancy couple. "You want to file a complaint, ma'am?" the shorter one asked. Mark was so close to me I could smell his fish dinner. I signed all the papers. Stevie stood next to me. He watched the officers handcuff his step-daddy and pack him into their car. Three days later, Mark came home. He locked Norma in the kids' bedroom and made Stevie watch what he'd made Mark do to me.

I begged Stevie: promise me you won't call 911 next time. But he refused.

"He's going to kill you, Mom," he said last week when I bent to kiss him goodnight. He'd seen my cell phone shattered on the floor. That made me sit up. There was a rhythm to our lives, a rhythm that I was used to, a rhythm that had recently sped up. But it could end. End with my children without a mother.

Now he stands in front of me, driven and unforgiving, more like Mark than I want him to be. He holds his black flute case tight in his hands. I nudge him out the door.

"Let's make cupcakes," I say, turning to Norma. "We'll

bring them to Stevie's school." Norma looks at me, incredulous. I can't believe it myself. I haven't made cupcakes in years. Norma helps me measure the ingredients. I find an old bottle of vanilla behind the spices. I let her stir. Our efforts make us feel daring. We open the thick curtain a crack, revealing a sliver of frowzy wet roses in our tiny backyard. Sunlight charges in as if it had been waiting patiently just outside the window.

At the kitchen table, I'm pouring batter into the baking pan, Norma licking the wooden spoon, when a raspy voice calls from outside. "Helloooo!"

It's Ramona.

She's never come without warning or when Mark isn't here. I'm not allowed to go out front, so I go out back in my slippers to the narrow side yard. Norma follows me, haltingly, still holding the spoon. I haven't seen Ramona since Stevie's birthday last year, but here she is, her salmon-colored perm springing from her head. In one hand, she holds out a box wrapped with bright blue tissue; in the other, a small paper bag.

"I feel like the Wicked Witch of the East," she says to Norma through the fence. "I totally missed your birthday, sweetie. And for you," she says to me, "lemons from my tree."

She shouldn't be here. But I don't send her away. I stay close to the house, hidden in its shadow. Behind her on the street, her car door is open like she's planning a quick getaway. Norma opens the gate and runs into her arms, knocking the bag out of her hands. Lemons scatter onto the grass still damp with last night's rain.

I don't want to go past the gate but Norma tugs me to the front lawn. The world feels too open out here, frighteningly wide. Ramona is squinting, the sun in her eyes. I squint too like any cave dweller. Ramona winces, then fixes it. She's never seen me without makeup: the bruises along the jaw, the dark around my eyes. I can't hide my cracked tooth or my oily, unkempt hair. I step back. I can't let her see me like this.

I once took pride in my sass, which came natural. When Mark and I first dated, we'd be driving down the street, little Stevie in the back moving his marbles from jar to jar, me humming an aria and looking out the window, when suddenly Mark would accuse me of staring at another man. "What if I was staring at another man?" I'd say. "There's a whole world out there and half of it is men. What am I supposed to do, big guy, close my eyes?"

But that cocky gal is long gone. I don't know what to say. Maybe something nice about Ramona's hair or the scarf, turquoise today, that covers her scar. The lemons look too yellow on the grass. I panic, dizzy with the clean morning air. It's been so long.

"Stevie has a concert tonight," Norma brags. "We get to go!"

Ramona doesn't seem to hear her. She comes in close. Too close, as if to study my skin. She's taller than me in her stacked heels. But I can see the horror in her eyes. Her face goes slack. She sees what I feel but can't ever say. Not just last night's bruises starting to bloom, but a faded map of bludgeoning, the darkness I hide, my libretto of pain.

"Margie," she says, so slow and deep I think her heart must

be breaking. She pulls me, or I fall against her, as if against a steep hillside. I feel her charitable bust and warmth, a repository for everything I've held in. The strawberry freshener she uses in her apartment is on her blouse and in her hair. Her heartbeat is a faraway drum in my ear.

"Can I open my present?" Norma says, pulling on my pajama top.

But I have no words. I'm the person Mark calls his *low-life bitch*, out in the front yard, sobbing now, without restraint, in his mother's arms. The birthday gift was just an excuse, I realize. Ramona came to see me. She strokes my hair.

I feel calmer now. In this quiet, tranquil world.

"I'm sorry for what I said about pity," Ramona says.

I'm stunned she remembers.

"It's you, sweetheart. Not us. My God."

"Look at my new dress!" Norma cries.

"What did *you* do?" I ask.

"I played it safe. I obeyed. It didn't always work. The drinking, the liver. I waited it out. The bastard died peacefully in his own bed—no fear or remorse, never disgraced."

She leans back so she can see my face again. She wants to explain herself. I don't need her reasons. "When the time is right," she tells me, "you'll know what to do." She crushes some bills into my hand. "Poor Mark," she says.

Norma tugs at my sleeve. I ignore her. I want to stay right here, in Ramona's arms.

———

The cupcakes are perfect, the frosting flavored with Ramona's lemons. I arrange them on a tray for the refreshment table and to protect them, lay a square of wax paper on top. Then I do what I never do. I open the kitchen curtain all the way and stand by the window. I let the midday sun warm my face.

I can't remember the last time I wore a dress, but I want to look good for Stevie. I find something stylish, a black long-sleeve sheath dress. I select a turquoise neck scarf like Ramona's, as if I too could disguise my wounds with a flash of silk.

While Norma naps, I shower. The bathroom is small, lit by a single bulb. Slowly, tenderly, I undress. Carefully, so that the fleece does not touch my skin, I let down my underpants, semen-stained and loose from last night. It is a relief to lay bare what I endure to the coolness of the air.

Today, I do not turn my back to the mirror over the sink. I bend in close, the porcelain cold against my thighs. I want to see what Ramona saw—how my jaw bleeds beneath the skin, how my forehead is marked with tongue-colored shapes. I take my time. I study my shoulders, my upper arms, my torso, all permanently discolored, a savagery of browns and blues. I search for my true skin color visible like patches of sky where the storm has broken. My breath wets the mirror. I am too close but how else can I see along the lips, the nose, around the eyes, scattered like seeds, the tiny constellations of scars, the dark eyes holding everything the mirror doesn't see? I marvel at my breasts, pale and pure, as though they belong to someone else's body. I step into the shower and draw the curtain.

Last year there was an incident. Our next-door neighbor called 911. That time I was ready. As soon as the cop car was off our block, she gave me forty dollars and a map to her cousin's place in Murrieta. I packed a rental car full of clothes and sheets. I strapped in the kids. I will never forget that feeling behind the wheel, speeding down Interstate 5 like a criminal, that shit smell coming from the feedlot near Coalinga. I rolled the windows down. I sang to the fields and the fattened cows. I planned to take my kids to the San Diego Zoo—lift them onto my shoulders for a better view of the fat white polar bears reclining on their stones, and the giraffes snapping off leaves.

But two weeks later, we returned to our shelter to find Mark on our front stoop. He claimed because of me he was a better man. And because he was a better man, he'd sue for custody of Norma if I didn't come back, or if I ever left again. And he would win. He didn't want to humiliate me in court. He begged me to come home instead. There was nowhere I could go, he reminded me, where he wouldn't find me.

I pull the curtain aside and step onto the bathmat. Norma is in the doorway.

I grab a towel, but she has already seen me. I go to her with one thought only, to somehow shield her, but I also want to smack her silly eyes shut. My palm against her skin makes a horrid sound.

Norma screams, then becomes so silent I'm afraid she'll never speak again.

I kneel to hold her. Her stringy pigtails stick to my damp

shoulder. I hate myself. I know how vile it feels to be comforted by the offender.

"I'm so sorry," I say. I promise her I'll never do it again. But I know I will.

I remember Stevie at the front door this morning like a lieutenant, giving me orders. The lives of my children unfold in front of me as if a technician were assembling them now. We are all in danger. Maybe that's what Ramona had meant last year.

One of us is going to die.

Mark knocks on the front door promptly at five. He has the key but he likes me to let him in. I rush to open it. I am ready for him in my black dress and scarf. "Ooh-la-la," he says and carries the week's groceries into the kitchen.

"Good news," he says. "They made me salesman of the week. I made so much I bought you this." He holds out a necklace with crimson stones. It's the most beautiful necklace I've ever seen. I'm flattered, bewildered. I put it on.

"Wow," Norma says. Thank God the redness on her cheek is gone.

"Look at the dress Grandma brought me," Norma says. But the visit was supposed to be our secret. I close the oven and turn slowly around.

"My mom?" Mark says. He uses his professional salesman voice, the one he rehearses in the dresser mirror. "Did you invite her here?" he says. He knows I couldn't have. I have no phone. But the bullfrog in his jaw is hopping in its little box. "What the fuck's going on here?" His voice suddenly high-pitched and raw, like a dog whose leg just got run over by a car.

On my toes, I kiss him on his neck the way he likes me to, a soft brush of the lips. I can't let him ruin everything now. The strategy could backfire, but he doesn't resist. I thrust my tongue inside his mouth. I rub his chest while the children watch. Mark knows exactly what I'm doing and so do I. He won't let the kids down, but later tonight when we're alone again, he'll do what he wants with me.

Soon we're at the table. Norma prods her chicken.

"I can't eat," Stevie says. He points to his tummy.

"You'll get that scholarship," Mark says. He gives Stevie an encouraging pat. "You've been working hard for it."

But Mark seems nervous himself, wiping his brow, dropping his napkin, like he's the one going on stage. I guess we all are.

At six thirty, I tell the children to put on their coats.

"Don't forget the cupcakes," Stevie says.

"You look pretty," Norma says to me. What she saw before is covered now. It's as if I have two bodies.

Mark opens the car door, first Norma's, then mine. Stevie sits behind me, wearing his white shirt and red orchestra vest. He rests his hand on my shoulder, its weight a comfort. Norma holds the tray of cupcakes carefully on the lap of her new pink party dress. Out the window, the houses look like toys.

Mark pulls over a block from the school and parks the car. He gets out and opens Norma's door. He lifts out the cupcake tray and rests it on the hood while he puts on his sport coat. I get out on the passenger side. Norma skips over to me. I reach for the tray. Behind me, Stevie closes his car door.

"I'd like to be the one to carry the cupcakes," I say.

"I've got it covered," Mark says.

But I have the tray now, safely in my hands. I've pictured it this way all along.

Mark takes it, not expecting me to hold on. He yanks it out of my hands. I smell the cupcakes' sweet, lemony scent as they pitch into the air.

"Daddy," Norma yells.

They tumble in slow motion before landing in the gutter, each little cake split inside its pink liner as if tossed from a high building.

"Mommy and me made those," Norma says. She's crying now. "*We* made them," she says. "We made them special."

Families walk past on their way to the concert. They stare.

"That's enough, kitten," Mark says, bending down to her height. Yellow frosting clings to the stitching on his shoes.

"Do you need help?" someone stops and asks. I look at the man. I wonder, in this afternoon light, if he can see the carnage in my eyes, if perhaps he might be the one who can save my children.

"No," I say, "everything is fine."

"I'll buy you any cupcake you want," Mark tells Norma. He takes her hand but she pulls it away. I don't know where Stevie is, then I see him huddled in the backseat of the car. Mark takes my arm. I straighten up. I have to for Stevie. Mark grabs Norma's hand hard so she can't escape.

"Get out," Mark says to Stevie. "We're doing this for you."

We are a family going to a concert. We move together in a clot toward Stevie's school.

Once at the auditorium, Stevie runs ahead to join the other orchestra students. Mark gets us programs. Plates of cookies and fancy cupcakes cover the PTA table. A gaggle of moms stand by the cash box with their perfect teeth. They look older than me. I picture their homes, curtains open, plush with light, their bodies under their pantsuits smooth and pure as stone.

Mark buys Norma a vanilla cupcake with an enormous swirl of green frosting, which she refuses to eat. He eats it himself.

Then a petite woman with a PTA pin on her lapel walks right up to us with that same kind of cupcake balanced in her open palm. She bends to Norma and offers it to her. Her hand around Norma's waist, she looks up at Mark.

"I saw you flip your daughter's cupcakes into the street, Mr. Bolton. Is that any way to behave around a child?"

I hear the words in Mark's head: *What are you, bitch, some kind of fucking social worker?* I see him flinch—an electric jolt.

But he smiles and says, "You're absolutely right, Mrs. Chenery," something he never says to me.

A successful life insurance agent is tactful, he has told me—the agent has to listen in a way that earns the client's trust. He claims he can get his clients to see precisely why they need what they do not want, even when they're dead set against it.

Mark is clever. And tough. But Mrs. Chenery is tougher. He's not invincible.

Norma licks her green swirl and clings to my leg as Mark regains his bearing and leads us away from the refreshment table.

Unfamiliar children are playing tag in the hallway. No one comes up to me and says, *Oh, you must be Stevie's mom, such a talented boy.* Or, *You look so glamorous, dear, in that dress, but if you don't mind me asking, why are you wearing sunglasses inside?*

Through the double doors, the auditorium looks huge, crammed with families, mothers chatting, fathers herding younger sisters and brothers to their seats. The ordinary world. I hold Mark's arm to steady myself.

The lobby lights flicker. Mark guides Norma and me to our seats. Norma sits between us holding the program in her lap. Mark reaches his arm across so he can rest his hand around my neck. The music teacher announces "American Salute." The orchestra is twenty fifth graders in red vests. I listen for Stevie. I let the melody cradle me: *When Johnny comes marching home again . . .* First drums, then brass and violins, then flutes.

When they announce the "Overture to *Norma*," Norma grabs my hand.

"Just for me," she says.

"Just for you."

The overture begins with its familiar brash chords followed by a scurry of violins. I close my eyes and let the music carry me into the opera's second act, "Mira, o Norma," the unforgettable duet between the High Priestess Norma and her young confidante, Adalgisa, who doesn't yet know they're both in love with the same man. Norma has just learned Pollione plans to desert her and their two children and return to Rome with Adalgisa. In the duet, she tells Adalgisa she too loves Pollione and the young priestess vows to persuade him to return to her, an act of such impossible sacrifice and loyalty, it breaks my heart every time. Lost in the story, I almost miss the sweet notes that are the prelude to Stevie's solo.

My son stands from his seat in the flute section. He is thinner and taller than most of the other boys. I lean forward. Tonight, in the dark, I hear his familiar breath inside the notes. At first, they waver like shy children, then find their way, beautiful and pure. He does not falter.

When the concert is over, two fifth-grade music camp scholarships are announced; one goes to Stevie. I jump to my feet. I can't help it. The three of us holler and clap, Norma standing on her chair. Stevie bows and squints into the glare. I see him see me. I see his pride.

Mark surprises us. He's arranged to go out for drinks with the principal, leaving the three of us to walk the eight blocks home without him.

Last night's rain is still in the air, the wetness clinging to the lawns. But tonight, the sky is clear. Stevie and Norma hold my hands and we do what we have never done. We walk down our street together without Mark. "This must be the Golden Age," Stevie says. We swing our arms and Stevie hums the "Overture" and Norma tries to copy him and all the arias I haven't sung are fire in my throat.

———

At two a.m., Mark knocks. No matter how late it is, he wants me to come to him. I make him wait. I poke my head into the kids' room. They look peaceful beneath their mitts and pucks. I've packed their backpacks and hid them in the closet by the front door. I have no clear plan.

Mark knocks again, louder. Slowly, I disengage the lock. When he enters, he nearly falls against me. I brace myself. I smell the vodka first, then the laundry soap on his shirt.

"Ready for me?" he slurs. As drunk as he is, he remembers our bargain.

You'll know what to do, Ramona said.

I grab Mark's car keys from his coat pocket.

"Yes," I say, "of course."

All the lights are off and I keep them off, thankful tonight for our blackout curtains that keep out the streetlight. The living room is darker than a cave.

I hear him get as far as the couch and collapse.

That's when it comes to me. The flute. I take Stevie's case from the chair where I'd left it in the entryway and sit on the far side of the living room. I unfasten the latch. I can barely make out the three silver-plated pieces nestled in velvet. I work quickly, by touch alone, fitting the head to the body, lining up the tone hole with the first key the way Stevie has taught me. I wet my forefinger and brush it against the tuning slide, then swivel the foot joint where it fits into the flute's body. I pry out the pad beneath the B-flat key. With one hand, I balance my weapon on my shoulder. I use D-sharp as my sight.

Mark's breathing is uneven. I can just make out the bulky shadow of his head, which slowly lifts and swivels, unable to locate me.

"Where are you?" he says. "Turn on the fucking lights."

I take my chances, taking my stance in the shadows halfway across the room.

"Mark," I say. "I've got a gun." His body goes still.

"Are you crazy, Margie?"

"It's loaded," I say.

"Don't mess with me," he says. "I've got the key." He lays his head back down. "Come over here, honey," he says. I hear him unbuckle his belt.

I'll take his car. We'll be four hours away before he can rent one. I've got Ramona's hundred-dollar bills in my back pocket.

I take the flute now in both hands, hold it in front of me like a rifle, and aim the barrel at his bulk. I press the B-flat key. Metal on metal. It makes a click, barely audible, but in the silence he hears it. I do it again.

"What in hell?" he says. His voice is strained, no longer the pissed-off Mark or the sweet-talking salesman Mark. I can tell he's afraid.

"Your mom gave it to me," I say. The lie comes as a revelation, stronger than any weapon. "Norma's dress was a cover-up."

He tries to sit up, falls over on his side. He did this to himself.

"You're both fucking bitches," he says, a drawl. But then something sinks in. I hear him fisticuff the couch.

The G-sharp lever is my trigger. I hold it down. At the end of the last act, the High Priestess Norma takes Pollione's hand and walks with him into the Druid's flaming pyre. But I'm not willing to die for love. I feel calm and strong. Like I can do anything. I almost forget to wake the kids and herd them out the door.

"No false moves," I tell Mark, like I've heard it on TV. I train the flute's imagined crosshairs on where his heart must be. Each time I fiddle with the lever, he moans.

"Norma, Stevie," I call out to wake them.

"Not the kids," Mark chokes out. "Not in front of the kids."

I take a step closer. I want to see the terror in his eyes, the thing Ramona never got to see.

I hear Stevie's slippers in the hall, then Norma's shuffling plastic pajama feet. I slowly back toward the front door.

"Where are you, Mommy?" Norma says.

"Keep the light off," I say. "Stevie, open the front door."

As soon as he does, a sliver of streetlight pierces the entryway.

"Take the car keys," I tell Stevie and throw them to him. "Grab the backpacks from the closet."

"I'm sorry," Mark tries to say, but he can't. He's throwing up now.

Stevie is at the threshold holding Norma to his chest.

"Hurry, Mom," he says.

But I can't help it. I want the movie to pause right here in this lit frame, Mark cowering and begging on the living room floor. I take three steps upstage and press the barrel of my weapon

into the side of his head like he's done to me. I want him to feel
the cold bullet chamber. It's only an instant, less than a second,
but I feel it, that tight space opening between my mouth and
my throat. Not a song, but the emptiness a song might fill. The
breath. The swell.

NIGHTLIGHT

Reiner slid his screwdriver down the door frame until he hit the deadbolt, pissed that he had once again given in to his wife and was actually breaking into their neighbor's house. The old widow, who had lived there alone, had died four months before, but yesterday evening, parking the car, Beth had noticed a suspicious light, "a lamp," she had said, coming from the basement apartment.

"What if there's a burglar in there? Or a crazy person? One tossed cigarette . . ."

She didn't have to say it. Flames would rip through their conjoined wooden houses faster than any fireman could strap on his hat. Reiner had scoffed at her suggestion to call the police. In the tiny German farming village where he'd grown up, people took such matters into their own hands.

Still, he had tried to avoid the unpleasant task. "Maybe it was just the moon's reflection in a mirror," he had said. But Beth persisted until he agreed to investigate.

Now the wind stung his face and cut at his neck. He tried thrusting the screwdriver in at different angles, but the bolt refused to budge. In the distance, St. Peter's bells rang out more times than there were hours on a clock. Beth and six-year-old

Marlowe had just headed there for Sunday Mass, the two of them skipping down the sidewalk in their dress-up coats.

"We'll be back for lunch," Beth had called out gaily as she escorted their son onto a path she unabashedly believed would one day lead him through the Pearly Gates. The small boy, lagging, had waved one last time, then vanished with his mother around the corner. As Reiner wrangled with the latch, he felt a lurch in his gut as if his wife and son were really gone, as if he had already lost them.

He glanced toward the street, quickly scanning the rows of prim San Francisco Edwardians on either side, struck, suddenly, by the fairy-tale quality of the two identically constructed facades in front of him, his and the old widow's, the one tidy and brightly trimmed, the other in near ruin. Convinced the street was empty, he heaved his bulk against the old widow's front door. It jerked open a few inches and stopped short. Reiner squeezed his head in. The living room was crammed floor to ceiling with stacks of moldy newspapers, unidentifiable items in plastic bags, a clutter of gutted cardboard boxes. Everywhere the black confetti of mice.

He covered his nose against the stench and shoved his body in, kicking the door shut behind him. Inside, everything seemed to be stirring. Shredded curtains fluttered in and out of ill-fitting windows. Faded photos lifted into the air and were tossed like tiny kites. All last night, the west wind had barreled down Twin Peaks and rammed Reiner's house with so much vigor the entire structure seemed to shift its weight. But here, where joists had weakened, nothing was protected.

Reiner pressed through the towers of rubbish, afraid he would run into some vile thing—a dead cat or rat—but the hoarding he found was worse. Memory upon memory never dispatched. A desk lamp with its dangling bent arm, a herd of analog TVs, porcelain men in striped pants, a human tooth.

Down the narrow hall from the living room was a child's room. Monopoly, Clue, Parcheesi pieces lay strewn over scattered piles of 1940s Newbery books. Off to the right, a plastic crate had been stuffed with children's shoes: ballet slippers and cowboy boots. Among them, a pair of scuffed white baby dress shoes with laces, identical to the ones he and Beth once bought for Marlowe. He thought of his son now, sitting at catechism, his hands folded in his lap, reciting his answers. The boy must be straining to grasp the same doctrine Reiner had had to memorize as a child. Salvation, as fact. The certainty of mercy and redemption. All a grandiose lie. One day he would tell him.

Methodically, Reiner inspected each room of the abandoned flat, feeling more desolate. The more impenetrable the clutter, the more dogged he became, as if the circuitry of his mind were embedded in the grooves and surfaces of the old widow's things. In the kitchen, See's candy boxes sat stacked on countertops. One was open, the oxidized chocolates snug in their little crenellated cups.

At the back wall, he discovered a door rusted shut. He shouldn't have leaned against it; it sprang open. If he hadn't grabbed the jamb, he would have fallen thirty feet. This must be what Marlowe jokingly called "the nowhere door," the second-story door that once led to stairs down to the widow's backyard. They could see it from their back balcony. The collapsed landing and stairs lay now in shambles below him as if sliced away from the house.

Off the kitchen, on the wall of a dark stairwell, Reiner was surprised to see giant letters scrawled in black. He touched a ragged *b*. The ink was still wet. Alert to his original mission, he listened, but there was no sound or sign of who had done it. More baffling still, he realized, stepping back and seeing the sentence in its entirety, was that this was a Heidegger quote from *Sein und Zeit*—he recognized it even in translation: *What is still possible: thinking that seeks to grasp the truth of being, starting from the monstrous site to which we find ourselves riveted.*

At fifteen, he had read and reread the famous book in the attic of his father's Rheinhessen farmhouse, unreservedly taking each sentence to heart. Now here Heidegger was, his postulation appearing in the widow's deserted house. Reiner laughed out loud at the absurdity of it. Then fell silent, overcome by the grim irony of the quote itself. Yes, here it fucking was, *the monstrous site,* the relentlessness of decay, the insidious dullness that settles in. He was literally standing in the thick of it. The once-cherished words felt threatening now, as if the house were taunting him, or the great philosopher himself were calling him out for having squandered that sliver of hope.

"What *is* still possible?" someone said behind him. Reiner spun around to see a kid in his late teens, almost as tall as Reiner but nearly half his width, his dark hair short and jagged as if he had cut it with the dull blade of a knife. He seemed to have many layers of clothes. All black.

"Who the fuck are you?" Reiner asked.

"I was about to ask the same thing."

"I live next door. But you—"

"Let's just say I've got a lifetime lease." He was grinning, missing some teeth. He extended a hand. His fingernails were long and oddly yellow, buffed with grime.

"Federico," he said. He smelled like mildew and stale sweat. "German, right? I hear the accent." He came closer. "They say Germans know Heidegger better than NASCAR drivers know Daytona."

"*You* wrote that?" Reiner said, incredulous, pointing to the graffiti. No one at Reiner's nanotech company talked about anything but stock options and the latest thriller. At home it was God's grace, Pokémon cards, and coupons. But not thought. Never an Idea. Over the years, Reiner had replaced the poetry and philosophy books he'd once kept stacked on his night table with *Nano Letters* and the *Journal for Nanophotonics*.

"Personally, I always felt Heidegger was wrong," the kid said. "But the idea intrigued me." He lit a cigarette. "Who knows? There probably *is* no escape from the monstrous site. Look at all this crap. But what do I know? Maybe there is." He threw the match to the floor and put it out with his bandaged foot. One tossed cigarette, Beth had warned.

"You can't stay here," Reiner said. "My wife—"

"Hey, it's winter, man. The place is empty."

"How'd you even get in?"

Reiner's left shoulder ached from ramming the front entrance. The back had no exit.

"If a pencil fits under a door, so can a mouse. No collarbone. Collapsible rib cage. The only limitation is the skull."

"Come on, man."

"The side alley door was unlocked."

Scheisse. There it was: Reiner cursed from birth to do everything the hard way. Or against his will, which was equally punishing. Plowing his father's field with a hoe when he could have used a tractor. Taking up engineering when math was his weakest suit—Beth had convinced him to give up philosophy for engineering so they'd "own more than two spoons and two plates." He'd forsaken his country, rented a house beyond their means in the neighborhood where Beth had grown up and taken a job he didn't really want, stacking graphene layers into carbon nanofibers in Silicon Valley with its grueling commute, in order to pay for it.

St. Peter's bells rang the hour, less strident this time. A call to noon Mass.

"Look kid, if I were you, I'd get the hell out of here by tonight."

Reiner worked his way back to the front door, anxious to exit the *Sturm und Drang* of the dead woman's house and return to the composure of his tree-lined street. But once he did, the row of identical houses looked fake, the scene as dull and flat as a still life. Reentering his home, waiting for Beth and Marlowe in their well-appointed living room, he had the strange sensation that he, too, had been painted there, a tall, sturdy, successful man relaxing with *Der Spiegel* on his couch.

When Beth returned from Mass, she looked ebullient, carrying her prayer book under her arm, her cheeks flushed from singing.

"Did you find anything?" she asked after sending Marlowe to his room to change out of his church clothes.

Reiner looked down at his large hands. If he had believed, once, that it was possible through thinking to escape the bane of existence, to slip through the gap of what he wanted the world to mean and what it was, he didn't now.

"You were mistaken, Beth," he said. "There is no danger."

That night, Reiner took out his clothes for the next day, aligning them on the rocking chair so it looked like he was sitting there. Button-down pale blue shirt, khaki pants, and the Nikes that hadn't yet succeeded in making him feel American.

Beth, who volunteered to sing old favorites to cancer patients in the hospital while Marlowe was in school, was in bed leafing through a Bloomingdale's catalog, her cropped black hair framing her face. She tended to jolly her mind with high heels one moment, the valley of death the next. After a few glossy pages, she would open her Bible to the psalms.

Reiner had met her when she was a tourist at the Weihnachtsmarkt in Frankfurt ten years before. A petite, outgoing woman, she had convinced him to come hear her sing at

St. Leonhardskirche and Liebfrauenkirche, where she had been recruited to be a soloist in their choirs. He would have followed her anywhere then, smitten by her translucent voice and its unexpected vigor, which seemed to saturate the foreboding cavities of cathedrals with its sweetness. Reiner would sit in a back pew, eyes closed, and let her soprano carry him to a pure and simple place, a place unburdened by the thinking mind, fraught as it was with the conundrums and entanglements he had been laboring for years to parcel out.

Meanwhile, Catholic dogma was Beth's bedrock. Back then, Reiner had found solace in her steadiness and optimism. But she had become increasingly pious over the years, even evangelical, insisting, for example, that he kneel during Marlowe's baptism. Last fall, she had registered the boy at St. Peter's, rather than public school, over Reiner's objections.

"What's wrong, honey?" she asked. She had a sixth sense for his melancholy moods. But this was more complicated than sadness. How could she understand what he'd felt prowling through the morass next door, or the way Heidegger's words had stirred him?

"Did you read the Chekhov?" he asked. The request felt urgent tonight, no longer a favor.

Beth put down her magazine. *Stories of Anton Chekhov* lay on its back on her nightstand, a coaster for her water glass.

If she would just read them, perhaps she would appreciate the crassness of his rural childhood, where books had been objects of contempt. After all, Biebelnheim was no different than Chekhov's Russia a century before: tractors plowing the vast flatlands at twilight, crows plummeting into the dormant fields in winter.

"Start with 'The Huntsman,'" he said, extracting the book from her nightstand and handing it to her. "It's only five pages."

"I bet someone always dies in these stories," she said, holding the book to her chest. Ever since her sister had died of cancer at ten, she'd been unable to tolerate suffering except in the Book of God. She yawned now, settling back on her pillows and setting the Chekhov on her nightstand. "I bet someone always leaves."

She was right. Reiner, himself, had departed the family farm at seventeen. He'd plowed his father's two hectares of sugar beets one last time, steering the bright green tractor in large concentric squares at dusk, the light shifting indelibly until, by the time he'd worked the field to the center, the entire world was dark. There, under the first few stars, he had felt as if he had already left it all behind: the fermenting air; the clean horizons; his mother's lingonberry pie; his father's twinkling, circumspect eyes, feet up in front of the television; his glum sister. The next day Reiner had packed his satchel with his favorite books and left for Frankfurt in skin-tight jeans, driving his clunky red Ford, a thin blond ponytail trailing halfway down his back, to study philosophy at the university.

"There's no special truth in your books," Beth said. "Nothing that I haven't already felt just living my life. And the women? I bet they're all dull. Or foolishly in love."

Beth's confidence often spooked the words right out of him.

He clicked on his reading lamp, turned off the overhead light, and joined her in bed, scooting close enough to feel her warmth. He'd been with her the morning Marlowe was born, holding her hand as she, on all fours, bucked and moaned. He had howled, Beth later told him, when his son emerged, viscous and full-formed, from between her legs, an eerie sound that had seemed to come from the earth's thermal core. He often recalled that moment, the way life itself had taken him by the throat. The next day, sitting next to his wife in the maternity ward, their tiny naked son asleep on her breast, there had been a timeless beauty to her exhaustion. He had almost felt inclined to believe in her merciful God.

He turned to her now, lifted her nightgown under the covers and slid his hand up to her hip. He felt an erection coming as he stroked the exquisite smoothness of her thigh.

The ceiling light clicked on.

"I heard a dog barking," Marlowe said, squinting, making his way to Reiner's side of the bed, pointing toward the wall that abutted the deserted house. His PJs were a frenzy of blue and green cabooses. He smelled faintly of sugar.

"It probably just heard a raccoon scrambling over a fence," Beth said. In their neighborhood, the doddering nocturnal animals were common.

Reiner took his son's hand and together they listened to the night. The dog started up again, its yelp an ecstatic pitch. Reiner lifted the flashlight from his nightstand, opened the French doors, and stepped out onto the narrow balcony. Shining the light on the house next door, he saw only dismembered two-by-fours and peeling paint. The brazen squatter must have left.

"Why is the nowhere door open?" asked Marlowe, suddenly next to him, staring at the back of the abandoned house.

"Go back inside," he said. "I'll take care of it."

"Come here, honey," Beth said from the threshold. Marlowe balked, then disappeared into the folds of her nightgown as they withdrew into the house. In bare feet, Reiner lumbered down the back stairs, the wood smooth and cold, made his way through Beth's thorny roses, and peered over the fence that separated the old widow's yard from his own. The kid had left the door ajar in the narrow alley that opened to the street on the first floor. He smiled, recalling Federico's quip about collapsible mice.

He turned back, but as soon as he did, the damn dog started up again with its barking. It wasn't until he had managed to hoist himself over and was well into the old widow's backyard that he caught sight of the "suspicious light" coming from deep inside her garden-level basement apartment. The boy *was* still there. Through a broken window, Reiner could see his lanky body angled awkwardly, apparently to retrieve enough illumination to read his book. A studious kid come in from the cold. Not the monster Beth had feared. What was he reading? Reiner wondered. What was he thinking? What harm could there be in letting him stay?

"You were right," he told Beth, a bit out of breath when he got back upstairs. "Raccoons. A whole family of them."

Reiner gave Marlowe a reassuring kiss on the top of his head and scooted him to bed, then edged toward Beth's warm body. She pulled down his tight boxers and sweatpants, lifted her nightgown up to her neck, and placed herself on top of him. Her desire absolved him. An ardent man, he took her into his arms.

But the next night, Reiner couldn't sleep, speculating about the homeless kid next door. He eased himself off the bed without waking Beth, threw on his robe, and returned to the old widow's backyard. Despite the cracked window, the teen looked comfortably at home. An itinerant breeze tousled his hair as he crouched under a blanket smoking a cigarette, intent on something in the dark. The following night, when Reiner checked again, he was gone. Reiner panicked. But, moments later, he showed up on a dilapidated bike carrying a burlap bag of what looked like cans of food and placed them carefully onto makeshift shelves inside his encampment. On the third night, he seemed to be reciting poems. Reiner squatted out of sight and listened, enchanted by the rhythm of the kid's voice, straining to make out the words. Was it Celan?

The tableau next door became more captivating each time. It seemed to Reiner that this homeless kid had taken Heidegger's *Sein und Zeit* to heart, the way Reiner once had, but this guy was the real deal—free to do nothing but eat, shit, sleep and think himself into Being.

In Biebelnheim, rodents scuttled through the fields at night, black-bellied hamsters, the size of a young child's shoes. Already, at nine, Reiner had not been like the other boys who loved to kill them. His father teased him for refusing to join in so he did, killing dozens of them with a trap that fit into their burrows and broke their necks. Twilight was the best time. The creatures thought themselves invisible. The little eyes gleamed. Reiner collected a dollar for each carcass from a tailor in the next town. It took the man three weeks to piece together a handsome cape with the miniature hides. The village priest promptly bought it for his kind, plump wife. She wore it on Christmas Eve.

And every day after that straight through Lent until the townspeople started sniping out of envy or boredom. Reiner assumed the entire village must have felt it, the bizarre beauty created from all those tiny deaths, this stunning metamorphosis of pests. But no one spoke of it. Young Reiner lay alone in his farmhouse attic mulling it over, but without the context or vocabulary such ruminations require. A few years later, that changed.

Returning home from soccer practice one afternoon at fifteen, he found his father—a head shorter than him by then—standing motionless in their garden in his yellow knee-high rubber boots, his upper body crawling with feral kittens. The setting sun lit the man's stocky silhouette from behind, etching his head and arms in a lattice of gold. Oddly, he tolerated the mewing creatures, the scene as beautiful as it was frightening. Here was the man who barked orders at him, who humiliated him, who slaughtered pigs and drank his own homemade *Eiswein* until he snored at the table, yet who today was a conduit to a liminal world, a mystical place that defied, incomprehensibly, the demands of a normal day.

"*Reiner*! *Komm zu mir*!" his father had called when he saw him, but Reiner, catching his mother's petulant eye in the kitchen window, walked past him and sprinted upstairs to his attic to reread the Heidegger chapter from *Gymnasium* that he hadn't understood. The philosopher's concept of Being in the World (*In-der-Welt-sein*)—a preintentional openness to true existence, one that would transcend the stink of sugar beets and his father's insults—suddenly made perfect sense.

That same month Reiner began riding his bike ten kilometers to the home of his philosophy teacher for late-night discourse. The two could spend hours debating the merits of a single phrase, like *Im Befremdlichen wandert*, the concept of wandering in estrangement, until his exhausted teacher, folding his rimless glasses and tucking them into their case, finally showed him the door. Reiner, elated, would ride home under the immensity of night's dome flushed by their surgical splicing of thought. At graduation, the elder man gifted him a signed edition of *Sein und Zeit*.

A week after breaking and entering his neighbor's house, Reiner arrived home later than usual from work. Beth was at a parent meeting at St. Peter's with Marlowe. He poured himself wine in a water glass, cut some of the country bread Beth knew he liked and broke off a chunk of cheese. Back in the living room, he was careful not to knock over Marlowe's latest train track configuration wending its way around the furniture. The boy was smart, but sentimental like his mother. He should have outgrown Thomas the Tank Engine by now. At Marlowe's age, Reiner was falling in love. He was sinking girls' pigtails into inkwells.

Reiner put the Spanish soccer channel on mute and propped his legs on the coffee table. After a day of stacking nanofibers, the sight of these little men kicking a ball back and forth on the green grass relaxed him. The red jerseys. The royal blue. The neat white numbers.

He had just settled in when he heard shuffling coming from the kitchen. Federico emerged from the darkness.

"*Was zur Hölle?*" Reiner said, scrambling up.

"The sliding door was open. No collapsible ribs required."

"You just broke into my fucking house!"

"Just saving you the trouble, man. Think I haven't seen you snooping around?" His voice was sultry with an accent Reiner couldn't trace, his eyes blacker than when he'd first seen him in the dimness of the deserted house. A silver pentacle with crossbones at its center dangled on his chest.

Reiner had a button on his cell phone. He could call the police.

"It's lonely over there," the kid said, strolling over to the bookshelf. "I thought I'd drop by while the family was gone." Was he spying? The bastard. The kid scanned the bindings on the shelf and pulled out Reiner's *Sein und Zeit* from among Beth's gardening books. "*Being and Time.* Just as I suspected." He opened it. "Impressive; signed by the old geezer himself."

"*Auf!*" Reiner said, snatching the book from the kid before he could soil it.

Federico glanced over to the mantel at the family photos.

"So there they roost," he said, picking one up in its silver frame—Reiner, Beth, and Marlowe on cross-country skis, hooded and smiling on a snowy slope. "'The most beautiful images,'" he said, putting the photo down in a different spot and settling on the couch, "'coalesce and then dissolve.' *You* know that."

The line was from Büchner. Reiner used to swoon over the young writer, valiant, prolific, dead at twenty-three.

Federico pulled a wrinkled napkin from his pocket and scribbled on it, then turned it over and scribbled some more, furiously, line after line, as if he were taking inventory or writing a poem.

"You must know Büchner's story about the young poet Lenz," Federico said, stuffing the napkin into his pocket. "That dude was terrified. The emptiness he felt was fucking excruciating. Remember how he hears that crazy singing coming from the hills and the walls of his boarding house? How blinded he was by his own mind, then exalted? You're like Lenz, Herr Reiner Eschenbach."

How did this snake know his name?

"That Büchner was one brilliant son of a bitch," Federico said.

The most beautiful images . . . Büchner's invincible words flaunted themselves in Reiner's mind, transporting him, just as they had done back in Biebelnheim. He hesitated. A crust of what looked like feces clung to the cuff of the young man's pants. He checked his pocket watch. Beth and Marlowe would be home soon.

But Büchner!

The kid sat there, picking at his nails, patiently looking up at him.

Reiner felt sheepish, one hand on his cell phone.

"'Only one thing abides,'" he finally said, reciting the second line of Büchner's poem in German, then in English. "'An infinite beauty.'"

"But what if the beauty is grotesque?" Federico shot back, swinging his legs up onto the couch. "Symmetry is not as sublime as you might think." He had no shoes. His feet were covered with strips of fabric wound and tied repeatedly into knots. Reiner knew he should tell the kid to leave. But he had to ask:

"What did you mean when you said, 'Maybe there *is* an escape from Heidegger's monstrous site.' Do you think he meant the human condition or a specific physical place?"

"I used to think he meant a real place."

"So did I. Fucking provincial Biebelnheim."

"How about that crappy basement in North Hollywood where I grew up? Manic mother, no father. Pretty monstrous."

"But wasn't Heidegger referring to something bigger?"

"I think he was referring to a place in the mind, some post-apocalyptic place, but before whatever might be coming next has even been born. I think the monstrous site is a kind of warning against itself."

"Yes, but he also meant emotions, didn't he? And mortality?" Reiner was sitting now on Beth's reading chair opposite the couch, leaning toward Federico. "When he said 'riveted,'" he meant 'fastened to,' but didn't he also mean 'fascinated by' our human place?"

Reiner caught a gleam in the young man's eyes, magnetism or hunger. He thought of Beth's carefully placed artifacts disappearing one by one at this young man's hands. But his mind was pulsing, the rusty spark plugs beginning to fire. He yielded to the irrepressible urge to put one hand on his heart, the other outstretched, and proclaim the coveted Greek words he'd not said in years: *"To gar auto noein estin te kai einai"*—thinking and being are the same—words he still believed to be true.

Federico laughed. "Fair Adonis," he said, "before you bleed to death on the tusk of a wild boar, how about some cash for a poor lost soul?"

But cash was too easy; nothing compared to these transactions of poetry and thought here in his house! Reiner felt himself grinning like a fool. Had this kid read Habermas, Adorno, Wittgenstein, men whose words he'd once raced upstairs to after silent meals in Biebelnheim, who later, in Frankfurt, had accompanied him to flea markets and cafés, his head throbbing with their discourse?

"What about *Öffentlichkeit*?" he asked. "The heyday of rational consensus in the public sphere. What's happened to that?"

Federico closed his eyes as if he were thinking and fished a hand-rolled cigarette from his pocket. Just as he raised it to his lips, Reiner heard his wife's footsteps on the front stairs and Marlowe's excited high-pitched voice.

"Scheisse," he whispered and signaled to Federico to slip out the way he'd come.

But Federico was in no rush. He rose languidly, proffering his filthy hand. Reiner yanked a five-dollar bill from his wallet and shoved it into the kid's fist. Beth was wrestling with the deadbolt.

"Hurry, damn it," Reiner said, herding him into the kitchen.

"Comrades?" Federico said over his shoulder.

"Get the fuck out."

Federico vanished through the sliding doors.

"We're home," Reiner heard Marlowe call from the foyer. The boy ran to where Reiner stood on the threshold of the dining room and took his hand.

"Guess where St. Peter's is taking us after Easter?" he said.

"What's that smell?" Beth said, hanging up her coat. She picked up Federico's cigarette from where it lay among chess pieces on the coffee table.

"Don't tell me you've started smoking again," she said.

Reiner stood dumbfounded, a billion synapses discharging in his brain.

"Lake Sonoma!" Marlowe shouted. "We all get to go!"

Later that evening, Reiner tucked Marlowe in and hurried to his study to search through the satchel of books he'd brought over the Atlantic. Büchner. Goethe. Schiller. Trakl. He hadn't looked at them since Marlowe was born. But tonight, the verses seemed to erupt, poems Reiner had mulled over month after month on a park bench in Frankfurt before losing himself in engineering exams and marriage. He recalled the words now—*Dichtung*—the feathery air, the angst he felt those days like small animals in his throat. He flipped now through the pages of a book and found what he was looking for, a quote about Celan: *A breach or rupture in the circle of the Rule,* his exclamation points in the margin still there from his last year at Gymnasium. Reiner had contemplated it then, the way a poem, an image, anything that pierced the boundaries of convention, could turn everything he'd believed to be true on its head. Like the rodent cape. Or kittens dangling from his father's jacket.

Things that cannot be yet are.

Without waking Beth, Reiner pulled a sweatshirt and loose jeans over his pajamas and opened the French doors onto the balcony. Wind shoved a regiment of fog over the city, everything the ocean didn't want. He descended the dark stairs, scaled the fence, and hesitated at the threshold to Federico's encampment, unsure what he would find, prophet or scoundrel, before pushing open the door. Federico was sprawled on the cement floor among candy wrappers, plastic water bottles, blackened bottle caps, an old tire. Moth-eaten blankets lay crumpled next to him along with a handful of hardcover books.

"What a hellhole," Reiner said. The ceiling was low, the walls damp; the air smelled of burnt milk.

Languorously, Federico pulled himself up, then air-boxed Reiner, a quick one-two punch.

"Like water, dude," he said, "we seek common ground." He

lowered one hand in a gesture of supplication. "No money, no bliss." He picked at a scab on his forearm.

"I just gave you money," Reiner said, dismayed that this kid had the gall to ask for another handout. But he handed him a ten spot. Federico kept asking for more until Reiner, as disgusted as he was enticed, realized he had given him everything in his wallet. In the nanorealm in which he worked, attractions and repulsions caused molecules to form intricate patterns, the kind that produce nanotubes in the cleanroom and snowflakes in the winter sky.

"'As I was walking up along the valley rim, I saw two girls sitting on a rock.' Do you know that one?" Federico said, stuffing Reiner's bills into a woolen sock. "'One was doing up her hair, the other helping her . . .'" As he spoke, he closed his eyes, tilting his head back, his face exuding an almost religious fervor.

"'And the golden hair hung down,'" Reiner recited, aroused by the words, "'and the pale serious face, yet so young, and the black dress, and the other girl taking such pains.'"

Federico patted Reiner chummily on the back.

"Now that's friendship," he said. He stood so close, Reiner could smell his breath, apples and cinnamon, probably a pastry someone had left in the street.

"How do you know Büchner? No one I've talked to here has even heard of him."

"I grew up poor. I know, like a billion other people in this lousy, fucking world. But my mother read to me. Yeats, Lorca. Celan's poems were my lullabies."

Reiner felt a pang in his chest. This kid had been spoon-fed literature. In Biebelnheim, he'd had to fight for everything he knew.

A distant siren caused Federico to freeze. The sound came closer, down the block.

"Shit," Federico said, scrambling into a corner.

Reiner instinctively shielded the boy with his heavy frame.

"No one even knows you're here."

"Shut the fuck up," said Federico. He cupped his hand over Reiner's mouth. It smelled like rotten fruit. Only when the siren disappeared completely did Federico take his hand away.

"What about your wife?" Federico said, holding up the culprit lamp so that the light was in Reiner's eyes. The cord was connected to a rusty hand-crank generator.

"She doesn't know."

"Oh, but she does. That woman understands more than you think."

He offered Reiner a grimy hand-rolled cigarette, which he took and Federico lit. Then he pulled a weatherworn blue Thomas the Tank Engine from his inside pocket and handed it to Reiner.

"I bet you don't know your kid waits for you every day at the window like a frigging lap dog. The minute your car pulls up, he ducks down. Give him a little something at least."

"What *are* you, some kind of family counselor?"

The two of them talked until dawn, meandering between the personal and the conceptual. They debated the origin of art and swapped stories about their mothers, one a nightclub dancer, the other a farmer's spiteful wife. Federico accused Heidegger of a reckless agrarian nostalgia. Reiner wondered momentarily if he, too, might suffer from the same. They discussed whether a poem should be inseparable from or unaffected by the torrent of history, laughed at each other's recollections of bad sex and deconstructed the concept of wandering in estrangement, until Reiner realized Federico was nearly asleep and he was the only one speaking.

Reiner had just stooped out of the kid's hovel when Federico called him back. "Words, my friend, may build a bridge into the world," he said, "but also into loneliness."

It was Easter, two weeks before Marlowe's St. Peter's field trip. Reiner sat in his usual spot at the head of the table, which was steaming with sweetness: Beth's mother's recipe for honeyed ham, potato gratin, and green beans with sliced almonds. Reiner was hungry after six weeks of being forced to endure Lent. Beth served the dinner. Marlowe was in the bathroom washing his hands.

"Where were you last night?" Beth asked, interrupting his thoughts. He'd been making stupid mistakes at work, small but critical, off by millimeters, costing the company. He had a meeting tomorrow with his supervisor for which he was devising a good story.

"Marlowe woke me up with a nightmare and you weren't there," she said.

He looked down at his empty plate, pressing his thumb and middle finger against his temple to fend off the headache.

"Tell me the truth, Reiner."

He counted on her being charitable.

"There's a homeless kid next door, Beth," he said. "He's cold. I brought him a blanket and a little food."

The week before, things had started to go missing out of Reiner's house. Little things that Beth hadn't yet noticed. Her blue Sheaffer pen, his Swiss Army knife. The betrayal had hurt. By then, Reiner was donating a hundred dollars a week for the boy's welfare. The kid was jeopardizing their entire arrangement. "I'll buy you whatever fucking knife you want," Reiner had shouted, "but I've got a family. My house is off limits."

"How long has he been there? Why didn't you tell me?"

"He's got nothing, Beth."

"I told you there was danger over there," she said. "I just knew it."

"He's just a kid."

"Then send him back to his parents, for God's sake."

"He reads Heidegger." But, of course, this fact didn't sway her. She carved the ham like she was murdering it.

"I bet that wasn't the first time you've gone over there." No mention of a tossed cigarette, their house in flames. Was she jealous?

"Someone's in the deserted house?" Marlowe called from the bathroom. He came in wiping his hands on his pants. "That must be why the nowhere door is open!"

"Join us in church if you're so hungry to talk about the meaning of life!" She tossed a slab of ham on his plate.

Marlowe walked over and attempted to nestle into his side. "Is he a sinner, Daddy? Will he hurt us?"

Beth gave Reiner her *I'll-put-an-end-to-this* look and proceeded to arrange food on each of their plates.

"Sit down," Reiner said, peeling Marlowe from his side and nudging him toward his chair. "Your food's getting cold."

"But I'm scared," Marlowe said.

"Sweetie," Beth said to Marlowe.

"You're coddling him, damn it!" Reiner shouted. "He'll grow up being scared of everything!"

Reiner remembered a better time.

Last year, they had rented a winter cabin. Around the potbellied stove, Beth had asked him to tell her his Biebelnheim stories, the funny ones he'd told her so many times and which she knew by heart—the way the priest's wife waddled to church tossing flowers like a bride in her hamster coat; how the butcher, sick of blood, became the baker of Rheinhessen's fanciest cakes; or that time Reiner's father found Reiner's sister's lost gold coin in the belly of a slaughtered pig—his mother cleaned it and served it on her daughter's pork chop, causing the forlorn girl to nearly faint with joy.

Early one morning, Reiner and Marlowe discovered a deer with two fawns not far from their cabin in the white meadow. For minutes, they stayed absolutely quiet, then Marlowe farted and they both fell back laughing into the snow. The deer family fled into the woods.

Last Father's Day, cajoled by Beth to join her large family at church, Reiner had joined the others at the altar when the priest requested all fathers come forward. He wouldn't have gotten up but Marlowe pushed him out of his seat. Standing before the large congregation, the choir singing hymns from the balcony, Reiner was surprised by the intensity of his own emotions, humiliated by the tears he couldn't hold back when he heard Beth's solo.

Reiner poured himself a full glass of wine and felt the weight of the silence. Beth seemed to begrudge her food. Marlowe moped over his plate.

"I'm sorry," Reiner finally said. He got up and put his hand on the boy's blond head. "No one's going to hurt us. I'll ask him to leave."

But by the time he returned home from work the next day, Beth had already called the police. She told him that night, once they were both in bed.

"I got them to board up all the doors and windows," she informed him. "They arrested him. I saw him, your young mind-mistress next door."

Reiner flung aside the bedcovers, threw his work clothes off the rocking chair in the far corner of the room, and sat down, glaring into the darkness.

"You have no idea what you're talking about," he finally

said. His despair swamped him, relentless as the fog heaving over the hills. "No idea."

Federico would despise him. Nothing frightened him more than jail.

But the next night, miraculously, Federico stood like a shadow on their bedroom balcony. He put his face against the glass. The only limitation is the skull, he'd said.

Reiner left a note on Beth's nightstand saying he didn't feel well and would sleep downstairs in the den so she wouldn't catch what he had. Then he went straight over to Federico's, who welcomed him with a bear hug.

"What did I tell you about your wife? Remember Büchner's Lucile, Reiner? That bitch stood at the guillotine with her husband's head bleeding on the stones and praised the king who'd just executed him!"

"You were right. I'm sorry." He patted his friend on the shoulder, which seemed to set him off, a dry, rattling cough from deep in the lungs. Reiner took off his jacket and wrapped it around Federico's shoulders. It was cold in the hovel. The wind swept through.

"I'll get you amoxicillin."

"It's too late for that."

"I'll bring blankets, then, but keep your damn light off until my wife's asleep. Be discreet, for God's sake." He settled onto the pile of old tires Federico had liberated so he'd have a place to sit, and felt his heart loosening, the way he'd felt it when he first saw the Heidegger quote upstairs in the widow's house, but fuller and far deeper now in this young man's company.

"Fucking pigs," Federico said, handing Reiner a cigarette.

"How'd you get out?"

"If you can roll a pencil . . ." They both laughed, Reiner so hard, he tumbled off the tire and fell against Federico, where he stayed, breathing in his friend's scent, mildew and cloves, and imagined what it might be like to be this free.

For the rest of the week, he made a show of sneezing at dinner, sipping the medicinal tea Beth brewed for him, then sneaking cash and cake and wine to Federico, always late at night. One evening, on the way home from work, he bought a copy of Celan's collected work and consumed *Der Meridian*, which Federico had recommended.

Standing in the doorway of Federico's hovel, he recited a favorite passage to impress him.

"'Whosoever walks on his head has heaven as an abyss beneath him,'" he said. "I love that line." His supervisor at work was threatening to fire him. Beth distrusted him. Everything was starting to make sense.

"But you, Herr Eschenbach, walk on your feet—which is why I trust you."

Federico turned away from him and bent over a Styrofoam cup, tearing at a cigarette filter with his teeth and spitting what looked like blood onto the floor. He pulled a syringe from his jacket and used it to suck up whatever was in the Styrofoam cup.

"*Dummkopf!*" Reiner said, standing.

"The best medicine," Federico said, injecting himself in his forearm.

"You're rotting your fucking mind." Reiner punched the wall, sick with the irony of it. The same dollars that gave him access to pleasure he had no longer thought possible were killing his only real friend.

The boy shuddered, grew flushed, broke into a sweat. Reiner couldn't watch.

"You fucking idiot."

He slammed the door and strode into the yard, where he stood for a long time in the wreckage of the old widow's back stairs beneath a bleary smattering of stars.

Reiner refused to bring Federico any more cash. Over the next few days, his friend became weaker, more desperate until he could barely sit up or talk.

"Dope sickness," he told Reiner. "Welcome to the real world, man. This is what it's like."

"I'm saving you, brother."

"You're no brother of mine."

That hurt. But the Celan and Büchner had all but disappeared. Against his better judgment, Reiner capitulated. He started doling out cash again in small amounts. But Federico began making impossible requests. He asked him for the password to his bank account. He begged him to stay all night. The day before Beth and Marlowe were to leave for Lake Sonoma, he insisted Reiner give him his copy of *Sein und Zeit*, which was out of the question.

"I thought you'd be loyal," Federico said.

"To you?"

"To your heart, Reiner. To that goddamn big heart of yours."

Federico put his hands around Reiner's wrists like cuffs.

"You can exist, Reiner," he said in that familiar, sultry voice he had. "The self-forgotten *I* can exist, just as you always suspected."

Federico's eyes were bright as if lit, like polished obsidian. Fever. Desire. He began coughing uncontrollably, lurching forward with each heave until he was kneeling on the floor.

Reiner bent down, extending his arm to steady him.

"You'll give it all to me soon enough," Federico predicted, once he caught his breath.

Early the following morning, Reiner and Marlowe kicked the soccer ball back and forth in the driveway. "One more time," Marlowe kept saying until Reiner finally lifted the gleeful boy onto his shoulders and carried him inside for their afternoon nap on the couch. As Reiner slept, he dreamt he was handing off a flailing, crying Marlowe to Federico, but was jolted awake by the high-pitched sound of children screaming and women's voices out on the street.

"They're here!" Marlowe said.

Beth came down from their bedroom with two packed bags, one for herself, one for Marlowe. Last night, she'd given Reiner an ultimatum. She'd seen the suspicious light. "I smell him on your skin," she'd told him. "You have a choice."

He couldn't look at her.

"Are you listening?" she asked. "I'm leaving for a week. We're your family. God knows we love you, Reiner, Marlowe and I. But there won't be a next time." She may have been thinking about her sister, the finality of premature loss. She looked right at him and he knew she meant it.

Yet now, as he walked over to her, she leaned into him, resting her tear-stained cheek against his chest, and he held her, startled, as he always was, by her radiant heat. She reached to stroke his head and he leaned into her hand like a cat. He desired her.

What is still possible.

He knew it was crazy, but he bounded upstairs to get the Chekhov. He saw her catch him slipping it into her bag. She actually smiled.

"Hi, Reiner," the field-trip moms said in unison when he came out. He held Marlowe's hand as they walked down the stairs to the sidewalk. "Work," he explained when Marlowe asked why he wasn't coming. More than half a dozen euphoric children squeezed back into the SUV. As the vehicle pulled out, Marlowe zigzagged Federico's little blue engine back and forth across his window and waved with his other hand until the car turned the corner.

Turning back, Reiner was again struck by the twin facades, his and the old widow's. Symmetry is not as sublime as you might think, Federico had said.

His living room looked golden in the late afternoon light.

Here were the overpriced couches and candelabras Beth had wanted him to buy, the accessories of a life that was still his. He paused before stepping over the latest train course Marlowe had built around the living room, surprised by the intricacy of his son's engineering. Had it always been this complicated? The boy seemed to have talent. Bridges, impossibly balanced, were sturdy enough to hold Thomas the Tank Engine and his loyal crew of cars. Switchbacks were frequent with no apparent beginning or end. What would he build next, at seven, at thirteen?

Reiner pictured the boy in middle school, his blond curls dark with sweat on the soccer pitch, Reiner yelling from the sideline, "Pass the fucking ball!" Where would the breach be for Marlowe? The rupture in the Circle of the Rule that would free him from the constraints of the material world? He would need to do better at steering the boy, not to lose him to decorum and doctrine.

Reiner slid open the sliding doors to their kitchen and stepped onto the back landing. For months, he'd never dared visit Federico during the day. Now there was nothing to stop him. He jogged down the few steps into Beth's garden, squeezed through the opening he'd made weeks ago in the fence, and rushed through the widow's yard to Federico's encampment, stopping short just outside the threshold. Huddled with Federico were two teenage boys in ripped denim and a girl in a short black dress. One boy was sweating profusely, shaking with tremors. The girl pulled a thin blanket over a swooning Federico. In the dimness, Reiner could see open sores on her arms. A wind came up, snaking through the wood slats and broken windows, rustling her dark uncombed hair, which fell to her waist.

He stepped back into the shadows, envious of these ragged kids' sharing of Federico and their ease together. Addicts, all of them. He felt as if he'd been struck. He was not like them, and yet he wanted nothing more than to be part of what they had.

One was doing up her hair, the other helping her. "That's friendship," Federico had said. And here it was.

"Reiner," Federico called, catching sight of him. He signaled to the girl, who drew Reiner down next to her and began to stroke him softly along the inside of his arm. She couldn't have been older than fifteen. She was wearing one of Beth's bracelets.

When Reiner got home from work the next day, the same girl was in his living room cradled in Beth's reading chair, wrapped in a towel, dreaming or sleeping, her long hair still damp from a bath or shower. The two teenage boys were nodding together in the leather recliner; Federico, shaved and in one of Reiner's white undershirts, lay on the couch. The gas fireplace was lit, though winter was long over. Federico got up and opened his arms, his skin blotched with track marks.

"Welcome home," he said. It had been Reiner who had suggested they camp out in his house while Beth was gone. Outside, the wind hurled itself against fences, walls, limbs. But here they were safe. If something was breaking, they could not hear it.

Reiner scanned the room for missing items, but everything was in its rightful place. He recalled a Trakl poem he had always loved, in which a man, walking down the street in the rain, chances to see a family through a window enjoying a meal around a table, the room dry and gently lit. The poem had always made him feel inexplicably sad.

Now he was at that house, standing at the front door.

Federico sat back on the couch. There were no bandages on his feet. He was wearing Reiner's socks. He looked quite handsome, the firelight playing on his face.

"*Alles Gute*," Reiner said.

"You're a fool, Reiner," his friend said. "What you see in front of you is an illusion. A fleeting dream. You think I'm going to be squatting next door forever? Your wife will kick me out. Or the house will get sold. And where will I be then? Huddled under a freeway ramp, that's where I'll be, my real home, digging cold beans out of a can, or lounging on some filthy sidewalk, mocked by tourists, spit on by some asshole in a suit, herded away by police. I'm grateful, man, for what you've given me. I truly am. But soon it will be summer. The sun will call us back to the streets." He took Reiner's hands in his. "But before I go, there's something I want you to have. You think I don't know what you were looking for the day I met you in your neighbor's house?"

He lit some tar in Marlowe's cup, Minnie Mouse primping immodestly on its side.

"You're wrong, Federico," Reiner said. "This is perfect—all of you here—just the way it is."

"Dude, truth isn't some fucking hobby. Something you pray

for on Sundays at church, or mainline weekday nights with some shifty squatter next door. It's a way of life. You've either got the courage to find it, or you don't."

When Reiner was seven and his sister nine, the two of them had wandered from their parents' farmhouse at the center of their village, walking together at twilight along the cobbled street. They soon came to the edge of the village where the fields and translucent skies spilled out before them. Reiner remembered that feeling: frightened by the vastness yet excited, too, to be at that precipice. His sister looked at him, quizzically, as if she expected something from him. As he stepped toward the darkening horizon, he heard her behind him: "Let's go back." She hurriedly took his hand and the little row of stucco houses with geraniums and pinwheels at the sill, along with everything he knew and understood, had been there to welcome them.

Screw the fucking geraniums. Reiner sat down next to his friend on the couch and forced himself to relax. This time he wouldn't let anyone call him back.

True friendship, Heidegger had said, is essentially a form of truth, and poetry, the essential conversation. But only with someone who cares what the essential conversation is. Beth had never known Reiner in that way. She couldn't know him. But he and Federico could—in Büchner's transgressive words—smash their skulls open and tear the thoughts from the very fibers of each other's brains.

Reiner rolled up one sleeve. In an instant, Federico had his upper arm wrapped with a spliced cord and the tarry liquid entered his blood, a warm rush as if someone had turned on an electric blanket everywhere under his skin. Federico blurred. Reiner's bliss spread, enlarged, consumed him. He heard Federico's voice, an incantation:

"'But I have held another cloth instead, / Coarser than this, no stitchery or seam.'" Reiner had learned the Celan poem by heart, Federico's favorite. *Rührst du's, fällt Schnee im Brombeerstrauch.* He wanted to recite the lines with Federico, but he was collapsing into himself without space or time. He couldn't speak. Federico's breath was a comfort against his skin. The danger, Reiner thought, is thought itself, Heidegger's *Ort*, winding unpredictably through the understory of the darkest woods. What a pleasure it was to let go of it.

Reiner's cell phone rang. The number on the screen was Beth's.

He didn't answer it. Closing his eyes, he imagined he was lying on Federico's old army blanket next to the nightlight in the squalid room next door.

The phone rang twice more. Federico watched him. They all did.

On the fourth ring, he flipped open his phone.

"You're home."

"*Was?*" he responded in German, the room seeming to spit out strands of light.

"Reiner?"

It was his wife. His wife.

"You should have taken off work, Reiner, and come! We

toured the lake in a restored schooner. Marlowe got to go fishing. He misses you."

"When are you coming home?" His throat felt like paste.

"Marlowe caught his own salmon. We all had it for dinner!" Reiner put his hand over Federico's mouth. His dark angel was starting to sob or laugh, he couldn't tell which.

"Reiner. What's that noise?"

"Soccer," he managed to say. "Munich."

"Thank goodness you're home, sweetheart. It's over, isn't it? Marlowe wants you to take him fishing this summer."

Reiner sifted through what felt like burning rooms in his mind, but could not locate anything but happiness.

Federico and the others were asleep when Reiner woke the next morning. He felt small and sick. He meant to wash up but faltered at the bathroom sink. So this was it. The apotheosis. "And what if the beauty is grotesque?" Federico had asked. Or desire strained too far. Marlowe dropped from the eagle's talons. And Beth, too, like devoured field mice. He couldn't bear it, not to kiss on a whim the top of his son's head. He thought of the old widow's photos of her children, hoarded and then dismissed. He felt the bruise on his arm swelling beneath his fingers.

He dressed and drove to work. But the following day, he didn't. Or the next. In the comfort of his own home, he talked and smoked and drank the black milk he'd paid for.

———

At the end of the week, Beth and Marlowe got dropped off late in the evening, rugged with camping. Reiner had been frantic all day, sweeping, wiping counters, bathtubs and floors, spraying air freshener so liberally it moistened his thin hair.

"I'm tired, Daddy," Marlowe said, looking up at him at the front door. But it was more than fatigue Reiner saw in his son's eyes, something neither Jesus nor Beth's pampering could soothe away. Reiner knelt down to the boy's height and held him.

"My God," he heard Beth say from the living room behind him as he carried Marlowe upstairs. "He was here."

Reiner sat on Marlowe's bedroom floor and sang "Stille Nacht" to him as he had done almost every night since the boy was born. *"Ich hab' ðich lieb,"* he said, and repeated the words even though Marlowe was asleep, then stayed there in the dark listening to his son's breathing. He felt the weight of it on his chest. How close he had come. Tomorrow, he would practice goal shots with Marlowe in the backyard.

He resisted getting up, but finally got himself to the master bedroom and sat in the rocking chair. Tonight, there was no wind. The whole world seemed silent. Not even a siren.

Beth came into the room with a stack of unused camp clothes and stood in front of him. Her eyes, more familiar than his own, had changed, as if carved deeper to hold grief.

"For God's sake, Reiner. For God's sake."

"What?" He had no idea how much she knew.

"Look at yourself. You're pale as death. You've given it all away."

She left him there and disappeared into the bathroom.

Reiner closed his eyes and fantasized how he would undress her. He would move his hands up her legs, running his fingers over her midriff and up to her breasts and she would let him. He would ply her with his Biebelnheim stories, one after another, the way he'd done so many times over their years together, the amusing ones she loved and the ones he wished he had already told her: how, as a boy, he always stopped what he was doing every time church bells began ringing in *heims* near and far, dozens of them, unsynchronized, animating the air; about those ecstatic evenings biking home from his professor's house beneath the stars. About Being-in-the-World. Until the sun came up. Until she understood why he had done what he had done, how everything had turned on its head.

But he felt nauseated. He'd soon be trembling. He knew something about dope sickness now. On his shoulder, he felt Beth's hand, lightly like a bird.

"My favorite was the shortest one," he heard her say. "'If any peasant gets in with hunters or horse traders, it's goodbye to the plow.' Remember, Reiner?"

Of course, he remembered. Yegor says this to Pelageya, his poor, forlorn wife. Then she watches him tromp away from her and disappear in the dust.

Once the spirit of freedom has taken a man, Chekhov writes in "The Huntsman," *you will never root it out of him*. Reiner knows the story by heart.

"It's such a beautiful moment," Beth was saying. "And so sad."

Reiner had never thought of it as sad. The Count had directed the mismatch of Yegor and Pelageya, persuading them with a few kegs of wine.

"Yegor doesn't love her," he said. "He never did."

"But Pelageya loves him anyway. He pities her. But she's happy to just be sitting next to him by the side of the road. Remember, at the end? She gets on her tippy-toes to see the top of his little white cap one more time as he walks away. She's no fool, Reiner. She's in love."

Reiner wanted to touch her, but he didn't. He couldn't, his muscles slack with withdrawal. From the rocking chair, he watched her turn off the overhead light, slide into her side of the bed, and lie on her back. She looked small, her skin obscenely pale even in the darkness. By the time he managed to get up from the chair and lie next to her, she was already sleeping. Slabs of light raked across the ceiling from a faraway car coming up the hill. When he closed his eyes, he remembered a Biebelnheim story he hadn't thought of in a long time. The one about the bridge he had crossed uneasily with his father after church every Sunday when he was a boy, unsure if he or the river were moving.

TASMANIANS

> "We have a dream instead of a country."
>
> —NONA BALAKIAN

Mariam likes to get up before Cedric, just as the world is taking shape, and stroll in her nightgown and robe through their newly built home on Novato Ridge—her Shangri-la. Oh, how they soothe her, these rolling hills that stretch north and west beyond the tidy housing development—*like a pride of sleeping lions*, she's pointed out to Cedric—their tawny, muscular backs marked by scattered native oak and stands of towering eucalyptus. Since their wedding ten years before, she and Cedric have been renters, moving north from Glendale to Bakersfield, Bakersfield to Gilroy, Gilroy to Burlingame, each time putting more miles between Mariam and her childhood home, where Osan, Mariam's paternal grandmother, still lives with Mariam's mother. This move to Novato was their fourth—*and last*, Cedric warned—relocation north.

It had been a hard-won agreement. But sensible, too, to tap into their retirement accounts in order to finally buy their own house, a house without a history. Cedric would be forced to commute to San Francisco in near darkness. But Mariam, finally safe from the disturbing remnants of other people's lives—a child's sock stuck between wainscoting, smudges of carmine that could have been blood—would stop keeping him up at night. Their move would be a secret until they got settled so that ninety-year-old Osan would stop sending Armenian heirlooms, each one addressed, like a curse, to Mariam Baghdassarian, not Mariam Bryce. The spark in her marriage would reignite. In fact, it already had.

When the kettle whistles, Cedric joins her on cue, suited and scrubbed. He is a short British man, already sweating in the record-breaking heat. Mousy brown wisps float like a woman's veil on his head. It still startles her, his resemblance to St. Raphael, whose colossal portrait brought comfort to her as a child, sitting next to Osan in the pew. Cedric has that same gentleness, those same pouty lips.

Mariam pours black tea into two porcelain cups.

"It's so hot," she says, twisting her dark, unruly hair off her neck. "Please, can't we turn on the AC?" But she knows the answer. They must be frugal. That was part of the bargain. She raises her steaming cup in a toast. Furniture has been purchased with zero-interest loans and small down payments. Everything else is out of boxes and has found its place.

"To us," she says. "Free of Osan!"

"Free of our entire savings," Cedric says, pretending to wipe away a tear. Theatrical Cedric. But she knows how happy he is. He's had two months of uninterrupted sleep. Last night, he made voracious love to her and she to him. How good that felt. Perhaps she'll finally agree to have a child. He's been begging for one.

Cedric steps in so close behind her his shirt buttons press into her back. She smells his minty breath.

"*Hatz yev agh gisenk,*" he whispers into her ear, butchering the Armenian—*May we have bread and salt between us*—the traditional Baghdassarian words of trust and friendship that Osan demanded they recite at their Glendale wedding. Cedric's dour family had sat clustered together in the front pew of St. Mary's Apostolic in their prudish Yorkshire outfits, his mother's gray plaid skirt crumpling onto her swollen ankles, his father's dull suit brightened by the flimsy red and green ribbons that Mariam's uncle had pinned to his lapel. Mariam's mother, a widow, her lips red and glistening, almost stole the show in her broad-brimmed hat. With the *Sazandar* band playing, and every Armenian clapping, she escorted Mariam down the aisle, dancing the *harsnapar* as if *she* were the bride, while Osan, hard of hearing, sat hunched in a folding chair up front in the same boxy black dress she wore to funerals.

After the vows, Osan insisted Mariam carry the traditional blue charm with its evil eye in the palm of her hand. Mariam told Cedric she'd never be able to wash the frankincense from her hair. But, of course, it went deeper than that. Cedric didn't understand how freighted a fragrance could be, how a simple charm could break her heart. "I love that smell," he said, seduced, it seemed, by the *Sazandar* and *harsnapar*, even flirting with her mother.

"Off to the Nasdaq," he now says, flicking scone crumbs from his shirt. A junior broker, he makes cold calls eight hours a day. Mariam follows his car to the end of the driveway, their new ritual, and watches as his taillights disappear around a curve in the road. To the east, the darkness gives way to an array of pastels until the sun seems to lodge in the branches of the lone oak on the horizon. How orange it looks, too loose, as if it were going to drip.

Mariam, who doesn't have to be at her new PR job in downtown Novato until eight, has inaugurated her own morning rituals to keep her anxieties in check. Still in her robe, she sits on her small patio facing the grove of eucalyptus on their property, three dozen saplings and centenarians, and listens to the birds flit from limb to limb, tiny magical things. She has tried following their music, roaming through the trees, breathing in their pungent scent, but has never seen the singers.

A wonderful choice, the real estate agent had effused. *Your eucalyptus will protect you from the Diablo winds.* Cedric, while reticent at first, now praises the trees: *I could not have designed a more reliable safeguard for our investment!* he likes to say. But for Mariam, they are much more than that. Abundant with life—insects and birds thriving on thousands of tiny flowers, sweet with nectar—they are a buffer not just against the wind, but against the world.

Her reverie is interrupted by a Mexican ranchera traveling from the bottom of her hill. She tries to ignore it, but the music blares louder, lively and plaintive, accompanied by the sound of an engine before cutting off at her gate. FedEx, she thinks. It must be their reading lamps. But when she gets to the gate, the delivery is from Osan, to whom she expressly did not give her Novato address. The rectangular package is wrapped in a soiled *New Armenia Daily*, carefully taped, and securely tied with kitchen twine.

Osan began mailing heirlooms when Mariam married Cedric, instead of the nice Armenian boy next door, and moved out of Glendale. It started with small things that fit in a drawer: a collection of coins, some dating back to the Ararat; a leather-bound journal of Armenian recipes, dishes Mariam loved growing up. Each package contained a scribbled note with some cryptic advice: *Even sly fox fall in trap*, which always felt ominous, or an actual omen, something preposterous like C*eðric have car wreck, janig*, or *Fire burn your house*, or *You make chilð in November*, none of which had happened. Cedric hadn't understood Mariam's irritation: "And by the way," he said, "I'm with Osan about that kid. He'll be half-British!" *Armenian*, Osan would say. *American*, her mother would insist. Impugned with a century of blood, Mariam thought, which was why she'd decided never to have one. She envied Cedric, who'd crossed the Atlantic without a single memento.

Osan's sentimental gifts soon became an assault, the assault a bombardment. Each time Mariam moved farther away, bigger things would arrive, traditional Armenian dishware, Christian reliquaries, and ceramic oil lamps. Mariam refused to clutter her modest apartments and her marriage with relics of a culture that did not belong to her. She'd asked nicely at first, then pleaded with her grandmother to stop. But last year, Osan, suffering early symptoms of dementia, began sending personal items that belonged to Mariam's dead father—his Sinclair radio watch, his embroidered skullcap, the wooden cross on the silver chain he always wore around his neck—suddenly desperate, it seemed, for Mariam to remember what Osan feared she'd forget. The barrage only got worse when they moved to Burlingame, each gift more upsetting than the last: a pair of old shoes Osan claimed she'd worn to cross the Syrian desert after the Turks murdered her family, the Pazryk rug that had once held her father's corpse. Mariam's nightmares had increased in frequency, her moaning and restlessness waking Cedric two and three times a night.

"What I would do," he said as they packed boxes for their move to Novato, "is put the whole bloody lot on eBay. We could pay off our mortgage in a month."

But she hadn't. She couldn't. It would be like throwing away her own limbs. Instead, she lugged the unwanted objects with her once again, half of them unwrapped, and locked them in the main hall closet.

That evening, returning home from work, Mariam finds Cedric lying awkwardly on the thin white cushions of their living room couch, singing along to Radiohead. *You've been stuck in a lift. In the belly of a whale.* Right up to move-in day, Cedric had lobbied to furnish the empty rooms with overstuffed chairs and flea market throw rugs reminiscent of his Liverpool childhood, but

Mariam had insisted on Scandinavian sleek: discounted teak and glass, their sharp angles amplified by south-facing windows.

She holds up the offending package.

"The lamps?"

"It's from Osan, Cedric."

He sits up. He's wearing Bermuda shorts and a short-sleeved shirt covered with tiny boats balancing on the crests of waterfalls.

"That's impossible," he says.

"I just wanted a break, just a few months. It's what *we* wanted."

She drops the radioactive package on the floor and holds onto both sides of the doorjamb as if the house might crush her.

"The woman is stalking me, Cedric. How did she get our address?"

"Maybe she's telepathic? A witch?"

He tilts his head to the side in that abashed way he has.

"This is no time to joke!" she says.

She expected him to be outraged by the inexplicable invasion—her St. Raphael, who has always known how to comfort her, who has gathered her up and taken her into the folds of his robe at times like these. But he doesn't even seem angry, nor does he move from the couch.

Mariam kicks the Glendale package along the floor, out of the living room and down the hall—cursing Osan under her breath along with her complicit mother, before pushing the odious thing into the crowded cavity of the closet.

"I understand them, Mari," she hears Cedric call after her as she steps out onto the patio to breathe in her trees. "They don't want to lose you."

Mariam and Cedric lie in their underwear on top of their bed-sheet. It's too hot to make love, or even to touch. While Cedric sleeps, Mariam stares at the whirring ceiling fan and listens to the distant drone of the Diablo wind, comforted by the knowl-edge that their eucalyptus grove will keep them safe. Down the hall, Osan's latest package pulses in the closet. The digital clock flashes its green minutes. Mariam tries to resist. But like a horror movie, the package has tentacles that slip under the closet door, down the hall, and wrap around her wrist. She doesn't remember putting on her slippers or retrieving the key from its hiding place. When she unlocks the hall closet, a few heirlooms tumble out along with this morning's arrival, which she manages to catch in her arms. The others, she shoves back onto shelves, already stuffed with dozens of Osan's unsolicited gifts, some clumsily rewrapped, others never opened. With her fingernail, she cuts through the tape of the FedEx package, snapping the twine with her teeth. Inside the cardboard box, beneath a clump of rags, is her father's *duduk*. *The container of all sorrows*, he used to call it. Mariam lifts the ancient musical instrument from its bed of cloth.

Sculpted from apricot wood, its flutelike body is dark, its reed smooth and squashed like a duck's bill. Osan's uncle managed to smuggle it out during the winter of 1914 through Istanbul, along with old suitcases filled with relics, when he escaped with his family from the Young Turks' campaign of extermination. She grew up with its music, the strains coming to her now, fragments of "Sev Moot Amber," sad and ethereal, her uncle's *ðham ðuðuk* a haunting drone behind her father's oscillating melodies.

Every April, for the Day of Remembrance, relatives and friends would gather in the small Tulare County town of Yettem, everyone speaking at once in their mother tongue, the youngest children asleep in their mothers' arms. The instrument in her lap is the same one whose notes held them there in that tableau on the grass encircled by fig and olive orchards, the men, drunk on brandy and wine, quiet or crying, singing old songs, the women repeating family stories of loss in Armenian so the older children wouldn't understand. But sometimes, even as a young child, Mariam did understand.

Crammed into the closet with Osan's heirlooms, she feels the suffocating sensation she disliked as a child: her face crushed against her aunts' ample breasts, her uncles' whiskery lips—so much hair, the citrus smell of their skin. She raises the duduk to her lips and places the reed on her tongue. It needs only her breath. She doesn't mean to blow but a pitiful sound comes out. A moan. And with that paltry, haunting sound, her father's familiar scent, sumac and cardamom.

The more you try to forget, the more you have to remember what to forget, he used to tell her. The words never made sense, yet they troubled her. A lot of things about her childhood didn't make sense: Her father lifting rugs and taking down paintings to scour every wall and floor two and three times a week with Pine-Sol.

Osan's crossing herself in front of saints and doors and deacons. Habits and phobias her Armenian mother, born in Fresno, joked about or chose to ignore. Behavior no one would explain. Like Osan's fear of fire and her father's list of house rules to protect her. No cigarettes, no barbecues in summer, no candles in Osan's homemade birthday cakes.

By the time Mariam was a teenager, her father's ration of good days had already been spent. She came home late in the afternoons and found him sitting in the semi-dark. Sometimes she would join him, sitting quietly in a nearby chair, hoping he would say something, at least make an effort to account for his suffering. She understood even then, that no child of his would ever be forced to hear whatever it was he'd heard, born among the few Armenian men and women who had survived their exile through the Syrian Desert to Aleppo.

One afternoon, after high school band practice, she found the old house quiet. A pastel light bled through cracks in the drawn curtains, dimly illuminating Osan's trove of family relics. Osan, asleep in her rocking chair, trembled like a dreaming cat. Her mother was in Fresno visiting her parents. Mariam expected her father to be sitting in his chair in the living room, but instead she found him in the den, hanging from his belt, his deep-set hazel eyes still moist.

Back in bed, Mariam lies awake. She closes her eyes, but her mind is rife with images. In the hour before dawn, the ridge is quiet. But music starts to drift through the open windows from somewhere on her property, someone playing a duduk. She puts in earplugs, but still hears it, "Sev Moot Amber," its mournful melody like children weeping. She wakes up Cedric.

"It's coming from out there," she says. "From the trees."

"What, pet?"

"His music, the duduk. My father always played it just before sunrise. He's playing it now."

"For Christ's sake, Mariam. We made a bargain. Now you're telling me your dad is on our property?"

"Our bargain was no deliveries, Cedric. Our bargain was no Osan." She pauses. "Listen, can't you hear it?"

"There's nothing out there," he says. "Osan is your grand-mother, for God's sake." He tries to gather her in his arms. But Mariam resists. "Okay, okay," he says. "The woman *can* be a bit suffocating, I admit. And your house. The dark rooms, the pall. I get it. I felt it, too."

"But it's not in your blood."

"And you? You weren't even born. Can't you get that into your head?" Cedric is standing now, away from her, somewhere in the darkness. "You weren't there!" he says. "And your father wasn't either!"

Mariam's heart hurts with what her husband refuses to understand. She sees his silhouette in the moonlight. No saint. A small, ordinary man.

For days, Mariam refuses to speak, nor does Cedric attempt to cajole her. At night, the duduk music is gone. But between midnight and three, the ridge never sleeps. Raccoons ransack garbage cans along the steep one-lane street. Coyotes yelp and howl, a frantic crooning. The wind throttles the eucalyptus, then softens as it tangles in the tops of trees, finally lulling her to sleep.

A week after the arrival of the duduk, she wakes to the echo of sirens ricocheting through the narrow roads leading up to their ridge. The piercing sound gets louder. "Cedric," she shouts to wake him before running to the patio where she sees a line of fire trucks careen by, red lights flashing, their sides nearly scraping her gate, before stopping just beyond her house.

From the end of the driveway, she sees it: funnels of flame leaping into the sky just three houses up. The fire shifts erratically in the wind, eucalyptus after eucalyptus exploding as if wired with sticks of dynamite. *Fire burn your house,* Osan had warned. The sound is unbearable, a crackling blitz, then the roar of each new blaze. Everywhere, the acrid smell of smoke.

Cedric is suddenly next to her with a dish towel to hold over her mouth. They run toward the spinning, blinking lights and join the cluster of neighbors in their nightclothes, their faces gaudy in the spectral light. An army of firefighters in canvas jackets, carrying giant hoses, has broken up into smaller battalions. One battalion, having given up on the house, sprints toward the trees. Two others swarm the hills behind the house. Off to the side, a family huddles against the huge wheel of a fire truck, the father staring at the flames, the mother gazing into the darkness, two young children pawing at her nightgown. Something collapses inside Mariam, like the ceiling beams beneath her neighbor's roof. She convulses uncontrollably. She can't explain the force of her grief. No one was injured. It isn't even her house.

"Back," a firefighter yells to the growing crowd through a bullhorn. "Stay back."

Cedric grabs her arm and leads her, still sobbing, toward their driveway as the fire lurches north. "Everything will be fine," he says. He holds her as she cries. More fire trucks arrive. From their driveway, they watch the fire lunge and falter, suddenly igniting in places where no flames have been, then weakening once again as the wind dies down, until the last fiery arms drown in the night.

"That was close," Cedric says, as they enter their house. "Too close." But once in bed, he falls asleep, his arm a comfort across her breasts. If only she could follow him to that peaceful place. On the wall over their dresser, the red eye of the smoke detector winks. Scenes unspool with each red flash. Her neighbor's children, their faces damp and lit by fire. Osan's Anatolian home in flames.

Mariam puts on her robe and wanders through the living and dining rooms, feeling like an itinerant in her own house. Her furniture gleams with a patina of strangeness. Outside, ash covers their property like a light snow. She imagines her curtains igniting, windows swelling then bursting, she and Cedric dashing out before the roof succumbs. She takes inventory: the TV sucked in like quicksand, the teak dining chairs burning, the couch disgorging its meager filling in the intense heat. When she walks by the main hall closet, she smells smoke. Is she imagining it? Not outside.

Here inside her house. She tastes the bitterness in her throat. What if all of Osan's heirlooms were to burn down to nothing? One flick of hot ash. Fire would sweep through their house. The end, finally. Not just a locked door. It wouldn't be her fault.

But when she opens the hall closet, the heirlooms are unharmed. She takes a small package off a top shelf and unwraps it. Inside is the cherrywood bowl Mariam used when shelling peas for Sunday supper with her father. On one of his good days, he would sit with her on the peeling white paint of their front stoop before church, she in a blue pinafore and a crisp white blouse with navy-blue anchors on the collar, he in a woven green vest, his wooden cross embedded in the dark chest hair snarling from the unbuttoned top third of his shirt.

The two of them used to joke about their Armenian neighbors as they passed by on the way to church.

"I can smell Mrs. Palakian's jasmine perfume from here!" her father would quip. "Queen of the South Pacific."

"Mr. Mirzoyan's hat looks awfully hungry," Mariam would say, "with all that fur!" Sometimes they would laugh until they cried.

As soon as Osan came out of the house wearing her everyday dress, the churchgoers always stopped to say hello, horrified but also dazzled by Osan's parables and prophecies, which sometimes came true. *Your son will fail math*, she would say. Or *Your ex-wife will win the lottery.* Then Mariam's unflappable mother would come out wearing a paisley Jackie O–style dress tight in the waist with a matching pillbox hat. She'd tighten Mariam's braids with two yanks. "Don't you pay attention to Osan's ramblings, Mari," she would whisper, taking Mariam's hand. "Come along, Mrs. Baghdassarian," she would almost sing to her mother-in-law, before beckoning to her husband—*Darling* was what she always called him—taking his arm and heading to St. Mary's Apostolic.

Mariam takes the cherrywood bowl out of the closet and sets it on the glass coffee table, then reconsiders. Its ochre knots and grain clash with everything she has. With the fire trucks gone, the night is eerily still. But then, ever so faintly, she hears her father's music skittering across the air as if the construction workers had secretly ground his bones into the walls of the house. As soon as she returns the bowl to the closet, everything is a special, vibrating quiet.

The next afternoon, while grocery shopping after work, Mariam stops at the fire station to get advice on how to protect their house. The fire danger placard in front of the station has been flipped from moderate to high alert.

"Eucalyptus are Tasmanian weeds," a fireman tells her, defaming her beloved trees with a single word. "They're like giant matchsticks. It's the tar. With the heat and this wind, we recommend you cut down any eucalyptus within fifty feet of your house."

"Oh, boy," Cedric says, when she tells him. "I feel trouble coming." Half their trees were within fifty feet of the house.

The following night Mariam finds him lying naked on their

bed, the ceiling fan at maximum, reading a *Time* magazine special report.

"Eucalyptus survive on fire," he says, calling her over. "They always have." He's the kind of man who stops the car, even on a highway, to save an addled dog on the shoulder. Now it's the trees he seems intent on saving.

"What about us, Cedric?" she says, sitting down next to him. "They're Tasmanian. They don't even belong here."

"And what about me?" he says, giving her a peck on the cheek. "I'm a Brit!" Then he points to the article in front of him. "Look, Mari. There are reasonable solutions. They describe them here in detail. Fire ecology, for example, a slow controlled burn of the understory."

"But you can't control fire, Cedric, especially in this heat."

"Plan B. We roll up our sleeves and clear out the debris ourselves."

"We'd never really do it. You know that."

She goes to the dresser to determine what, if anything, is worth saving and places a few random items in a shoebox: a turquoise bracelet Cedric bought her for their fifth anniversary, a mother-of-pearl hair clip she bought last year in San Francisco.

"I'm uneasy with where this whole thing is heading," Cedric says behind her.

The next morning there is no wind. Mariam sits on her holy bench and waits for the sun to unveil the world. The lone oak on the eastern hill is shrouded in darkness even as the sky is lit blue and the vast yardage of a cloud unfurls its tints and texture. A neighbor's cat joins her on the patio, flopping onto the flagstone, then spreading out, impervious to human shame or fear or even to the songbirds, who soon start up, invisible among the eucalyptus, as if last week's fire never happened. Up the street, steam still rises from a cadre of blackened eucalyptus and the morning air is still tarnished with the stench of smoke. Already, the day's heat moistens her robe.

Something is working inside Mariam, hurriedly stitching itself, rhythmically, steadily, like a machine racing back and forth, its needle reinforcing a ripped seam, and then another one, and another, under her nightgown. It's as if the spool of thread were in her heart. She can feel it pulling.

Half of her trees could be tagged by the county for demolition. Slowly, they light up from the top down as the sun rises behind the hills, silvering their upper branches. Mariam leaves the patio and wanders into her grove for the solace she always finds there, but, instead, the Tasmanians frighten her with their grotesqueness. Close up, the older trunks are ravaged, stripped of their bark, the last fibers clinging to them like rags. Branch after branch is split at the joint; on the ground, detritus, decades of wreckage. The sharp, menthol smell coats her throat.

Mariam doesn't know who to blame: Osan, her husband, the wind. Night after night she dreams of fires igniting, smoldering lampshades, blackened coins, young children screaming in pain. She wakes Cedric, but he's convinced *butchering the trees* is not the way to go. He starts sleeping on the couch. "This is our last move," he reminds her. Together, they had agreed: the house would make or break them. He tries to reassure her, acknowledging her fears, but defending the trees. He suggests she get counseling. But Mariam's sadness is singed into her skin.

She stops rising before dawn. Cedric makes his own tea. Nothing about the house gives her pleasure anymore. At work, she is increasingly distracted. One night she dreams that the hall closet is a giant casket of charred bodies. She recognizes her father's limp hands in the jumble and wakes with a start, her heart beating fast. Cedric is singing in the shower. She comes into the bathroom and sees him, the shower curtain pulled to the side, his thin hair pasted over his brow by the strong showerhead.

"We can't wait any longer," she says as he steps onto the mat.

He comes toward her. She feels the heat from his skin before he touches her. But he doesn't touch her. He gives her a mock salute.

"Anything you say, General Baghdassarian," he snaps, snatching his bath towel and wrapping it around his waist.

"I'm scared, Cedric," she says, stepping next to him. She tells him about the estimates she's gotten, about Treemasters, a licensed company with competitive fees. She has called about a second mortgage.

Cedric turns to the mirror and brings his chin in close to analyze the damage of a single night's growth. While shaving, he bargains with her. They go back and forth in the misty light of the bathroom. It's too dangerous. What about a compromise? Okay, not fifty, just forty feet from the house. No? All right, thirty. Anything else, he says, seems too extreme. She agrees. But a moment later, she grabs his arm, causing him to nick himself.

"Dammit," he says.

"Feel my heart. Put your hand right here." She tries to lay his hand against her breast, but he pulls away.

"You know what, Mari? I'm up to my skull with saving you." He pitches his razor into the sink so hard it scratches the porcelain. "Do whatever the bloody hell you please."

He dresses quickly, zipping his pants, slipping his belt through the loops, rushing a misshapen knot into his tie. His face is half shaven. He doesn't say goodbye. He'll come around, she thinks. He always does. Once the trees close to the house are gone, she'll be calm again. The spark will come back. Cedric will be a father.

Mariam hears the tree trimmers before she sees them. Their truck motors groan in the distance and enter her open gate. In the driveway, the workers empty their trucks of machetes and chainsaws, three rusty blue generators, and endless lengths of rope. She steps outside. They approach in their orange Treemasters caps, the youngest one smiling, showing his silver teeth.

Mariam feels the stitching loosening inside her. With the morning sun in her eyes, she can't see the incendiary trees, all shadow and glare, but she knows they're out there. Her attempt to compromise with Cedric seems ludicrous now, the county minimum alarmingly insufficient. There will still be twenty trees on their property. They'll cross-pollinate. They'll disperse hundreds of seeds. New saplings will grow, each one as flammable as the next.

"I want them all cut down," she says to the foreman, her arm sweeping in a full arc.

"Are you sure, ma'am?" he asks. "It'll cost you. I'll have to send for more crew."

"All of them," she says.

Back in her living room, she hears the men dragging heavy equipment toward the back of the house, then calling from somewhere in the trees: *Hey-yeh! Pablito! Aqui está!*—then the buzz-shriek of a saw somewhere behind the kitchen. Then another so far above her house she imagines the smiling, silver-toothed boy must be dangling from the highest branches. The neighbor's cat runs from the patio terrified but Mariam feels the danger disappearing. She wonders if her father felt this way as he put his belt around his neck and stepped off the chair.

Outside, sawdust from the Treemasters whirls and sprays, sticking to the glass. Mariam walks in and out of rooms, shutting open windows, closing curtains. She fixes herself breakfast, but has no appetite. An hour goes by. Then another. Somewhere behind her, a machine starts up like an old car turning over, revving, resisting, then subsiding into a drone. There's the cut and then—is it in her mind?—a girl's voice coming from the same direction. *Their skin is gone,* she says in Armenian. *Their tummy sacks swell up like balloons. A young soldier throws me to the dirt. He kicks my head with his boot to put out the fire in my hair.*

Mariam runs to the window. But, of course, there's no one

there, just the workers. A felled trunk lies on the ground, its rings exposed, each concentric circle red and damp, a map of passed time. Is it coming from there? *There are a dozen soldiers,* she hears the girl say, *men in shiny black boots and gray fezzes.*

The Treemasters' cries are louder now, more urgent. Mariam hears the crack of timber. *Peligro! Peligro!* The whole house shakes when the trunk hits the ground. *We're thirsty from the smoke,* the voice is saying. *A nice soldier offers us water in a wide metal bucket. Mama kneels down. When she cups her hands to drink, he cracks her skull with the butt of his gun. A tiny sound comes out. Or is it blood? It lands in the dirt. I try to pick it up with my fingers.*

Outside Mariam's bedroom, the girl begins to weep. Mariam covers her ears. But she can still hear the machetes' blades, the roar and drone and hum and whine, the deep abrasive cry of one eucalyptus limb after another entering the chopper's mouth. She sees a worker hanging from a limb, cradled by ropes. More trucks arrive, more crew, munitions. A chainsaw starts up, just beyond the window, slow and constant, the old tree resisting.

She picks up the phone to tell Cedric about the girl, but stops herself. He won't believe her. He felt the pall, he said, but never the lethal darkness beneath that cloak, or the keening sorrow leaking from every painting, relic, and rug scavenged from the destroyed houses of Osan's dead relatives, then dragged to America, where they've cluttered every wall and floor of the Baghdassarian house for more than half a century.

Outside, the din comes to a sudden halt. Far overhead, Mariam hears the tiny roar of an airplane. The workers must be taking a break, relaxing in the shade of a tree they will later cut down.

She dials her home in Glendale for the first time in months. The phone rings and rings. What if Osan is dying? Maybe that's why she sent the duduk. Her mother answers.

"Is Tadik okay?"

"Of course she is, darling. Of course." Her mother is in her usual high spirits. "How is your new place? Tell me everything."

"I need to talk to her," Mariam says. She hears scuffling on the other end, then Osan's voice, thin and wavery like electricity in the air, but close as if there weren't four hundred miles between them.

"Mariam." A long pause. "I send duduk, janig."

She wants to scold her grandmother, but can't. She can almost smell the old woman's skin, fenugreek and thyme.

"There was a fire, Tadik. Just like you said. And now your voice is in the trees, your little girl voice. I'm sure it's you."

There is silence on the other end. Mariam hears her grandmother's wheezy breath. She pictures her in the ill-fitting dress she always wears, one strap limp, fallen off her shoulder, a faded kerchief over her frizzy blue-white hair.

"*Yes kez ga searem,*" Osan says too loud, as if it were Mariam who is almost deaf.

"I love you, too, Tadik. I really . . ."

"Make Baghdassarian child, you love me," she says before abruptly hanging up like she always does.

Mariam opens the hall closet. Shards of light filter in from between the drawn curtains in the living room. She picks up a small velvet frame, a sepia photo of her father as a small boy, holding onto Osan's dark skirt. Mariam looks at it closely, holding it up to the light. Osan must have been the same age Mariam is now. She has the same wild hair. Mariam touches the photo, then a lamp. Gripped by a desire to unwrap every unopened package, she rips open a copper box filled with a folded prayer cloth, then tears the yellowed newsprint from a framed print of Mother Armenia, a leather journal of recipes for *gata* and *madzoonaboor*, a set of blue bowls. There are too many things. She leans against the doorjamb, taking it all in. Osan's heirlooms seem innocent now in the strange quiet of the afternoon, almost restful, a jumble of odd beautiful things.

A large rug is balanced against the wall to the right of the door. She unwraps it quickly as if it might disappear in her hands. It is her uncle's Pazryk rug where she lay reading as a child, sinking into it as if its burnished reds could warm her on cool nights like the thermal earth, waiting for that special moment when Osan would call her to her lap for a story.

Mariam drags the heavy tapestry out of the closet and unrolls it, draping it like a flag over the white Scandinavian couch. A hundred suns decorate the border. Toward the center, a wooded landscape spreads out in an asymmetrical pattern of apricot trees and dark blue birds. Piano lessons at Mrs. Ozonian's house on the corner; birthday parties at Santa Monica Beach; laughing hysterically with Osan after burning the sweet *nazook* before Easter. These are not her father's memories or Osan's. They are hers. She collapses onto a chair and listens to the rhythm of her own slow breath.

Too soon, the crushing and grinding erupts again from somewhere in the canopy. *Más fuerza,* a worker yells. The grinding whines faster, then stops. She knows intuitively which tree it is: the largest eucalyptus on her property, stationed like a sentry outside her bedroom window. Mariam feels the tree's defiance. She hears that first moment when its circumference hits up against the metal teeth, then louder, deeper, followed by a guttural spitting whine, and then, out of nowhere, her father's accented voice, the one she has pushed and pushed away, close now, as if he were with her in the room. The words sound familiar, heard, perhaps, as a young child, incomprehensible at the time, but stored away.

Mama was so young, he says. *Behind her, the burning roof of her house caved in on her brothers and sisters. Her father, her grandparents, many of her cousins, their clothes already in flames, were led out at gunpoint, then shot, their bodies thrown in the front yard like a pile of old chairs. All night, the soldiers in their blue coats and yellow sashes forced Mama to stand guard over their charred bodies.*

Mariam closes her eyes against the ache in her heart. Her father must have watched over them himself, day in and day out, so Osan wouldn't have to, mourning the murdered with his music until he just couldn't do it anymore. She retrieves his duduk from where she'd buried it beneath other packages and sets it on her coffee table—a simple wooden flute, elegant and silent. She wants to show it to Cedric tonight. She wants him to feel the weight of it in his hands, to sit with him on the couch in the quiet of the evening, the Pazryk rug lying flat under the coffee table, and tell him things she has never told him.

She checks the kitchen clock. It's already four. She exits out the sliding door to the patio where she is shocked by what she sees. She runs to the driveway, past the garage to the top of the ridge where she can see her husband's tiny car winding up the road and the whole scene spread before her: the blank red dirt of their hillside strewn now with tree limbs and pith, decapitated trunks and half-cut trees, not one eucalyptus left standing. Everywhere the ubiquitous oil-blue haze. She smells the tart sap.

Pablito! O Dios! Dios! The boy with silver teeth is running up the hill toward her. Then the others. They are all running. They are calling out. She is frightened, but they are laughing. The wind, with little now to stop it, has made off with their caps.

THE HERMIT'S TATTOO

Sometimes I wonder why anyone is saved.

—BR. AUGUSTINE

The backroad that October night blistered with heat and smoke as it curved through the valley like a river. Behind me, the place of my silence. A place that was never itself silent. Nor had I been able to make it so. When I gardened or prayed or drew water from the well, I'd hear the wing-wind of the two resident ravens and their gurgling deep-throated calls, the rapid knocking of woodpeckers ramming thumb-sized holes into the lone telephone pole, the twitter of swallows and sparrows in the blue oak limbs. At dusk, the bullfrogs belched out their pain and lust like drunk bastards on a street corner. After my evening meal, I often sat on my deck and listened to their existential hollering: I'm here, I'm here, I'm here. Their insistence felt brutal. But I could imagine a time when they would not be here, nor would anything that survives on chlorophyll or a heartbeat. The land was loquacious. But not that night.

That night the valley animals were stunned mute. Blazing fires crowned the Sonoma hills to the north and east before sheeting downslope four hundred yards a minute, leaping over gullies and glens, fanned by Diablo winds. There'd been no rain in the land. *A drought is upon her waters,* wrote Jeremiah, *and they shall be dried up: for it is the land of graven images, and they are mad upon their idols.* The rapid knocking had been the fireman waking me from a dream, his helmet off, sweat clinging to his bushy brow. He was shouting, telling me to leave the hermitage that housed a decade of my prayers in its eaves. And as many misgivings.

How many times had I watched the fish in the lily pond dart and glide like the rapacious thoughts I attempted daily to replace with God's voice? I listened harder, knelt longer in my tiny chapel, repeated the solemn vows, which forbade me mourn or treasure her. But I could not shed the world. Until that day last spring when God Himself arrived, foot soldier and King, at my doorstep, and forgave my flawed call to holiness. He granted me, as part of His bargain, the ancient ritual of salabrasion, penance for having loved someone more than Him.

"Leave everything," the fireman yelled when I went to grab my Carthusian robe from a hook. There was no time to save my miniatures: Our Lady of Refuge and St. John on the Cross. My battered pickup rattled down the road between walls of flame. I thought of my two friends, the ravens who mated every year in a different valley, but always brought their brood to mine to feed and learn to fly. I fed them what I could not eat, leftover quinoa, and kale from my garden. They were sky animals. They didn't require superhero escapes from the blazes as did the brazen frogs, and the lizards, jackrabbits, coyote, voles, and wild boar. I hadn't smelled the fire as I slept, immersed as I'd been in my dreaming. A small town in New Hampshire. A little girl. A red tricycle buried in the snow.

The fireman hadn't meant to rake my wound, the skin red and raw beneath my nightshirt where I'd rubbed salt into my tattoo that morning in a third attempt to erase her name. The tricycle had gone missing from her garage, and I, at five, had found it for her that New England winter before the warmth of spring could beat me to it. She opened the door, her hair in two long braids, which she crossed against her chest without utterance. I have wondered if such *Kinder* love is supposed to endure, but it did endure—even when at twelve she moved away, even as I began to hear God's call. My heart, a red-hot crucible, finally cooled during my silent years at Grande Chartreuse hermitage in Grenoble, only to heat up once more my thirtieth year when I learned that she had died. *Stat crux дum volvitur orbis*. The Cross is steady while the world is turning.

A flaming tree fell across the road, barely missing my hood. The car in front of me backed up. Two young men, like gods themselves, jumped out carrying axes, split the fallen trunk, and heaved the fiery chunks to either side with their bare hands, risking their lives to save mine. Why had no one saved my childhood friend? At six, we dared each other to run under fat bellies of cows at pasture, sprayed each other with hoses in the middle of the street, climbed along connecting fences like raccoons as if we owned our cul-de-sac. At nine, we perched high in an elm and read Gunnel Linde's *The White Stone*, imagining *we* were the boy and girl with secret names. At twelve, lying on our backs in

the grass, she shared her flying dreams and as she spoke, almost
a song, I left the earth and soared with her over slopes of golden
birch and crimson dogwood, our town's tiny roofs and steeples
far below. *Blessed is the woman unto whom the Lord imputeth not
iniquity, and in whose spirit there is no guile.* She who had left me
twice, and now again, this last time, from my own skin. A quiet
child, I'd sat on the curb and watched her family pile into their
green station wagon packed to the roof with their belongings.

Chastity is the most radical poverty, Merton wrote. At word of
her death, I snuck out of Grande Chartreuse by cover of night
and walked to rue Denfert Rochereau where I paid an artist
to tattoo her name in large Gothic letters diagonally across my
chest, then hid the graven image beneath my robe. As I fled the
fire, I held the damp cloth the fireman had given me over my
mouth. *Cast all memory of the world behind you,* said Saint Bruno.
Your cell will teach you everything. Penance, I learned, is a process.
You must abrade the tattoo six times. Each time, the outer layers
of skin rub off. You bandage the wound. Each lesion takes eight
weeks to heal. Everywhere in the hills and valleys, sparks were
lighting a thousand spot fires.

The shelter was bustling with dogs and families, cases of bot-
tled water, Cheerios, respirators, and cots. I stammered when
spoken to and kept to myself. On the third day, in an outdoor
shower, a county towel wrapped around my waist, a young boy
saw the tattoo I was scrubbing out. "What's that?" he asked.
A crowd of children appeared, twelve of them, boys and girls,
all homeless now, astonished to see I had Chloe's faded name,

red with rubbing, writ large like a sash from my shoulder to my waist. "It's gone," I said. I'd drawn the ink out with salt. "No, it's not," they said. "It's there." That evening they followed me like kittens swatting at trailing yarn. Why are you bald? they asked. How old are you? Who's Chloe? And I answered them. I made pancakes for fifty people for three weeks straight. I told ribald jokes about monastics.

When I returned home in my pickup truck, it was to slopes of blackness. Any tree without charred limbs was an aberration. There were no hens crowing at the bottom of the hill, no finches twittering in the olive trees. Everything that hadn't burned had left. But my modest hut and chapel were still there, the Bible open to Psalm 32, just as I'd left it during my last evening prayer. Along the singed railing of my deck, I hung the damp boxer shorts and faded blue T-shirts that a family had donated to the shelter, washed and rinsed with water from the well. I sat facing east and watched the Strawberry Moon rise over the large metal cross on the hill that I'd mounted between stones the year I arrived. My chest, itself a cratered moonscape, would always hold Chloe's name. I slipped my hand beneath my robe and felt each letter, thick with layers of new skin. It wasn't the first time I'd been overcome. *The job of the monk is to weep, not to teach*, said Pope John. The Carthusians said, *Destroy yourself completely.*

Ash, it turns out, is an aphrodisiac for wildflowers and grasses. The dead amongst the living, the living living better than before. I made my potato soup and washed the pot, the bowl and the spoon. I waited in the valley's silence without expectation as the carbonized earth around me reincarnated into a sweet belligerent green. Then one day, one of the ravens came back with her four-foot wingspan and said, in raven-speak, I missed you, Br. Augustine, missed your quinoa and kale. The air-borne were saved and they came back, and perhaps because they came back, everything came back, the bullfrogs and rabbits and voles.

TRIPTYCH

For Seth

I

Grady Delacroix was a strange bird. That's what my son Cash calls him, not without love, now that he's six; a bird Cash understood as if they were born in the same nest, a bird the two of us could never quite catch. The day I moved in to the apartment next to his, six months pregnant with Cash, Grady, in his early thirties, immaculately dressed in blue jeans and flannel, announced he had AIDS, which was considered a gay disease back in '84. Even in San Francisco, most everyone believed the virus could be casually transmitted through saliva and tears. The CDC had come out with a contrary proclamation the year before but the scourge seemed biblical in its punishment and proportion.

I was twenty-nine, a budding artist and stubbornly single. The last thing I'd wanted was to have a kid. Yet I'd become oddly protective of my unborn child. For months, I did my best to avoid my infected neighbor, something I later came to regret.

The landlord had divided the first floor of his Eureka Valley Victorian into two inexpensive rentals: Grady's, a dark, cramped studio apartment that faced the street, and mine, a spacious garden apartment in the back with north-facing windows that gave me just enough reflected light to paint. Grady and I shared a wall.

One morning, a few weeks before Cash was due, I was checking the mailbox when Grady stepped out to water his potted plants. I pretended I hadn't seen him but he launched into a gruesome account of the San Ysidro McDonald's massacre with so much gusto, I thought he'd been there. Then he abruptly switched topic: a plane crash he'd seen live on the news, *One hundred fifty dead. Only one survivor.* He would do anything, he said, to meet that four-year-old girl, a miracle kid with third-degree burns. The parrot he'd inherited from his dead lover, he went on, had begun saying things no one had taught him: *Jesus Christ* as an expletive and *You look mahvelous* with a Spanish accent.

Grady talked fast, without breathing, like a magician pulling a chain of red scarves from his mouth. As he spoke, his compact body rocked back and forth. He said he'd been to General Hospital that morning to see his doctor, a dead ringer for Cary Grant in *I'm No Angel*.

"I'm his miracle kid," he said. "Like that little girl."

But that morning the doctor had stamped him with an expiration date: six months, "As if I were a slab of cheese."

I didn't know what to say. I'd never consoled someone who was terminal. I wanted to leave, but felt riveted to the spot. Grady squinted at me as if he expected me to conjure a cure. He was exactly my height. In the sunlight, his eyes were that teeming blend of blues I'd been trying for years to paint, too animate for a man who was dying. I, too, was wrestling with death, death at sea.

I leaned back, bolstering my belly with both hands. Cash circled inside me like a monkey around a branch. He was due in three weeks. It struck me then that neither Grady nor I had much time. I, too, had been granted six months. But for me it meant life. After years of gallery rejections, my first solo show was scheduled for March.

At the Art Institute's Alumni Biennial the year before, the gallerist from East & West, a small but reputable gallery in the Fillmore, had stopped to praise my paintings, a sampling from my *SS Arctic* series. "Reminiscent of Twombly's *Hero and Leandro*," he mused. "Exactly," I lied. He stepped back to regard my work in silence. "A jigger of deconstruction," he suddenly announced, "with a spritz of impressionism," as if my art were a cocktail. We signed a contract; one, we hoped, of many. I was to complete six new paintings for my show. Cash must have heard my curses and late-night laments from inside the womb. He showed up two weeks late. With the extra time, I managed to finish #*11* of the series, leaving me just two more to paint.

But on October fourteenth, my brushwork screeched to a halt.

My Art Institute friends flocked in, cooing like doves— *Ooooh! A baby!*—then vanished when the novelty wore off to curate downtown shows. Their careers were on fire, while mine, like damp kindling, was threatening to go out.

Weeks slogged by without sleep or a shower, my only sustenance scraped from a can. I diapered, pampered, breastfed, and bitched. My mother called from our hog farm in Kentucky. As a child, I'd loved those pigs more than people. "Come on home," she said, but I refused to get trapped again in the suffocating web of rural holy-rolling Mackville.

Six weeks in, I sat in front of *SS Arctic #12* with Cash squashed into a sling against my chest. The pulse on my neck must have mesmerized him. His tiny fingers kept reaching for the edges of my hair. I tried to ignore him. My large canvas was demanding cobalt blue. I picked up my brush. Cash banged my jaw with a wayward hand. I painted a long diagonal line. He cried. The line was too dark. I picked up a tube of titanium white. He spit up on my palette. The instant I pulled up my shirt, he rooted around on my chest like a feral kitten.

Cash had been feisty even before he was a fetus. Half his DNA busted through the Trojan barrier on the saxophonist I'd danced with at Club DV8. A home pregnancy test displayed the dreaded blue line. Apprised of the news, the sax player disappeared like a trill into a room full of smoke.

Keep the baby, my mother said. My friends weren't so sure. Choose, my gallerist said: diapers or paint. A counselor at the clinic asked me to close my eyes and imagine my life in ten years, in thirty, with child and without. Either way, I couldn't imagine it. I'd scrimped for years so I could finally paint full time.

But something happened on the way to my abortion appointment when I stopped at a red light. Cash—no bigger than a car key—managed to trick my Corolla into turning right toward home, instead of left toward the clinic, as if *he* were in charge.

Now here he was on my breast, as desperate for milk as I was for deliverance. I closed my eyes and switched him to the other breast until he was satiated and blissful, then picked up my brush, greedy to reenter my art. But Cash was both angel and thief. Even sated, he sucked and licked. It was impossible to concentrate.

I yanked him off my nipple and held him in front of me, a squealing piglet, when I heard a knock on my front door. If I believed in telepathy, I would have sworn it was the child police. I trundled down the hallway, my uncombed hair pale and stiff as pitched hay, and pulled aside the little curtain.

Grady Delacroix stood on the other side, jittering like an old car idling in winter. He held up two steaming red-and-white cartons of Chinese takeout.

II

While Llyn, nine months pregnant, waddled from room to room next door, Grady couldn't read or sleep or even smoke the weed he'd scored at the park. Not since his doctor had read him his last rites. Other than the gold-toothed cashier at the corner store, who was there to care? He was dying, for God's sake. He could live without final communion, but he ached for sacramental confession and the anointing of the sick, knowing no Catholic priest would get near him.

Week after week, he lay in the same bed where just a year before he'd nursed his dying lover—a hardy young man from

Arkansas—sponging and turning him until he took his last breath. The man hadn't been miraculous like Grady. He'd died in five weeks, bequeathing everything to Grady, who had been homeless when they met. Grady turned on his side and watched the dead man's angelfish float in and out of pink coral castles. Under the blue light, they looked like real angels. The king snake uncoiled in its terrarium as if it had all the time in the world.

You look mahvelous, the parrot said from his cage, tilting his head in the moonlight.

"Shut up, damn it," Grady yelled, surprising himself as much as the bird. He'd never been a cursing man. But the profusion of funerals had made him bitter. Night after sleepless night, every death he'd ever known came to mind, whizzing by like cars on a freeway. First the strangers—victims of natural disasters, armies, characters murdered in fiction. Then acquaintances—barbers and priests, octogenarians he'd done home care for, changing their diapers and grinding their pills when no one would hire him for anything else. Every lane was crammed with cars: three dead ex-lovers, dozens of friends and friends of friends, young men like himself who had, within months of each other, been vanquished by the pandemic.

There was no one left to talk to. With each passing day, he felt lonelier and more frightened. Not of dying so much, but at the prospect of Hell.

Last night, as the traffic zoomed by in Grady's mind, a fancy fifties Cadillac had put on its brakes. It was his father's car:

midnight blue, gray roof, whitewall tires. The passenger door
had opened, unleashing magnolia-drenched Assumption Parish
heat. His little sister lay on the vinyl seat.

Grady rushed to the bathroom, a room so small the sink and
wall held him up, bile rising in his throat. The entirety of his
insides seemed to come out. Hanging over the toilet, awaiting
a second heave, he heard Llyn's newborn howling in the next
apartment. The little bugger must have finally popped out.
Llyn would need him. He smiled, picturing the three of them
in Llyn's kitchen, a holy trinity, happily having lunch. String
bean chicken in oyster sauce would be his calling card.

That afternoon, Llyn answered his knock looking haggard in
an oversized shirt, its front stained with blue paint, her infant
wailing somewhere deep inside her apartment. She thanked him
profusely, opening the door just wide enough for him to slip in
the containers. But he came back the next day and the day after
that. He arrived with Szechuan lamb, kung pao chicken, mu
shu pork. Each time, Llyn opened her door a bit wider, until
she finally let him in.

"Please, can you take him?" she said. Her newborn was
tucked into a sling on her chest, too tiny to be human. Once
in the kitchen, she offered Grady a pair of yellow dishwashing
gloves before lifting her son from the sling like a rabbit out of a
hat. "You don't mind, do you? His name's Cash."

She quickly put the infant into his gloved hands and ripped
open the greasy takeout carton, closing her eyes and tilting her
head back as if to forever capture the scent. Grady moved to

sit down with her at the dining table but she pointed him to the fainting room in the back.

"Hold him carefully on your lap," she warned. "Keep him away from your mouth."

Grady absorbed her caution without reply. At San Francisco comedy clubs, it was not unusual to hear a stand-up bark at the crowd: *Those of you with AIDS, please raise your hands. When you leave, we're going to boil your chairs!*

Grady maneuvered his way through the large multipurpose room. An easel stood opposite the stove. Canvases, most of them blank, leaned against the rickety table and walls. A huge one, sloshed with the blue paint he'd seen on her shirt, was balanced precariously against a shabby couch. The entire place reeked of oil paint and turpentine. At the room's exit, he hesitated, but Llyn assured him she'd be nearby. Which is how he ended up alone in a rocking chair attempting to hold a baby for the first time since he'd held his baby sister. Not the holy trinity he'd hoped for, but a start.

When Cash's head slipped beneath his arm, Grady panicked, afraid the newborn would suffocate. He tried holding him against his chest but the baby's feet slipped out of his swaddling wrap or his head lolled. It would require four hands, Grady decided, to keep the baby from falling apart. He tried different configurations until he discovered that by curving one arm around the trunk while cupping his other hand around the back of the head, the baby could breathe, look, and listen, without any bones snapping.

"Come look at us," he called to Llyn.

"In a minute."

It was late afternoon. Cash's eyes, dark and unfocused, looked too big for his head. His arms and cheeks were a faint pink. Grady made a clicking sound with his tongue. Cash kicked his little feet inside his blanket, his tiny mouth working itself into indefinable shapes. Grady laughed. He felt the sadness rise through him like mist.

Since before she could walk, Grady's sister Eva had been as coy as his mother, flirting and teasing him, smelling of sweet clover. When she was two and he ten, she loved him to tickle her. *Stop*, she would say. Then a minute later, *Again.* By the time she was old enough for preschool, she was begging him to tackle her, gently, on the living room rug and tickle her under the arms, along the ribs, until she could barely stand it. He liked the feeling, too, her little pajamaed body warm and solid against him, squirming and twisting until he couldn't tell where he ended and she began.

Grady was the best babysitter in Belle Rose, Louisiana. His parents paid him a dollar each time they went out. He used to read Dr. Seuss, acting out the stories, egged on by Eva's laughter, until she fell asleep in her crib. But that summer night, she'd had a high fever and had fallen asleep before his mother left the house. His father, a storm chaser, was in Alabama photographing tornadoes. Grady had spent the evening in the cellar, masturbating to the men's underwear section of his mother's Sears catalog, then greedily reading the final chapters of *The Secret of the Old Clock*.

He must have languished there for hours before remembering his mother's instructions: check on your little sister. But it was too late. When he rushed upstairs, Eva was barely breathing.

Carefully, he lay Cash's heavy head on his shoulder and rocked him, but was soon surprised to feel the newborn sucking on his lower neck as if starving for something Grady had. Unnerved, he pushed both boots to the rug, abruptly halting the rocking and lowered the infant to his lap, gingerly, as if he were made of glass. Grady's limbs twitched involuntarily, yet Cash was strangely calm, listening, it seemed, through the open window, to the twilight cries of gulls and the murmur of wind chimes in the back garden. Grady leaned toward him so their faces were almost touching and closed his eyes, hoping to inhale his sister's familiar honeyed scent.

"Oh my God!" Llyn said, appearing at the threshold and whisking her son out of his arms. Cash wailed as if he'd been struck. The sound crimped Grady's heart.

"Get out!" Llyn said, bouncing Cash in a futile effort to quiet him. Grady slunk past her, navigating through her jumble of paintings, then down the narrow hallway and out the front door. Nothing bad had happened, yet guilt poured into him like wet cement. Once on the landing, he turned toward Llyn's kitchen window where she stood watching, her baby bawling on her hip.

III

At the funeral, you sit next to your mom in a plastic chair. You see two crows in a tree and four black coats in a pile next to the grave. The man with the shovel is sweating. In front of you, the headstone says: *Grady Delacroix, 1954–1991.* You know how to subtract. A pretty lady asks your mom why she brought you, like you aren't already here listening to what she has to say. He's too young, the lady says. She has big hair and a red stone on her finger. Her lips shine like spitballs in the sun.

He skipped first grade, your mom says. He understands more than you think.

The lady wipes away a tear. Grady came to my wedding, she confides, then bends down and kisses you on the cheek without asking. You wipe it away.

You're wearing a suit because your mom made you. And a tie and a crinkly shirt. Sometimes your mom steps in front of you to shake someone's hand and then you can't see the priest or the hole in the ground or Grady's doctor who doesn't look like a doctor because he's not wearing a stethoscope or a long white coat.

The man with the shovel lays it down on the grass. A woman in a flower dress flitters her hands like hummingbirds over strings and music comes out. Maybe she's an angel. Six men in dark suits carry a big box. The men put the box in the hole. That's where Grady is, your mom says. But you already know. A cloud passes the sun. Your shadow disappears. Up in the tree, the crows are noisy. With your brain, you tell them to stop and they do. You are a bird whisperer. That's what Grady said.

Now you hear Grady's voice. Not the tiny one that started to sleep in his throat, the long ago one that blasted out of him like boys' voices at recess. You felt something sad in his words before you knew the word for sad. Like that feeling you still get when your mom leaves the room.

Grady loved to tell stories. You never knew if they were true. He said his little sister was *sweet blue* so many times, you thought Sweet Blue was her name. She was in a little box on the table, he said, and everyone at her wake was sweating except her, even the mayor of the town. Grady's bare legs kept sticking to the vinyl on his chair. He lifted them up and down. He liked that sound, he told you, like ripping off a Band-Aid. Up and down. Up and down.

You little devil! his mean mom yelled at him through her teeth so no one else could hear. Go to your room! his dad shouted in front of everyone. Grady's house had fifteen rooms, but he didn't go to any of them. He watched the two sweat marks on his chair get smaller and smaller even after his dad gave him a whack.

Your brain switches like a TV channel and you wonder if Grady even knows you're here.

The priest is wearing a white dress and standing next to the big hole. He's saying words like *Lord* and *forgive* and you hear an echo even when no one is talking. Only the doctor has an umbrella when it starts to rain so you can't tell anymore who's really crying.

One day when you were almost four, your mom explained that bad bugs were killing good bugs inside Grady's body because the antibodies were saying, No, I don't want to help. You went and got your flashlight. You told her you would crawl inside him through his mouth and fight off each of those bad bugs yourself!

You're a champ to want to try, she said.

But you couldn't save him.

Your mom takes off your suit jacket and puts it on your head. But you take it off. You want to be wet.

IV

I had no desire to paint the tilted stern or the miniature lifeboats overloaded with male passengers. What fascinated me was the acre of ocean where the women and children went down. My mother's father used to sit me on a stool in front of his armchair and tell me the story his father had told him. The SS *Arctic*, heading to New York from Liverpool, took four hours to sink after it collided with a smaller vessel fifty miles off the coast of Newfoundland. In the chaos, only the crew and able-bodied men had survived, the ship tragically supplied with rafts and lifeboats sufficient for less than half the 400 passengers. My great-grandfather's parents had perished along with his five brothers and three sisters.

Just seven at the time, my great-grandfather had survived, together with the ship's captain, clinging to the starboard paddle box. He'd seen desperate men lash together anything that could float—chairs, caskets, sofas, and doors—while a young man fired a cannon at one-minute intervals, hoping a ship was nearby. He'd heard women and children, 250 of them, stranded on board, singing hymns as the giant ship slowly sank, then seen them shivering and scared in the cold water, huddled like mice, his own mother and brothers, heads tilted back, eyes glassy and empty, grasping at each other's limbs, trying to breathe. He'd been surprised by how fast they'd disappeared, by how quiet death was. No one screamed. My grandfather must have told me the story of his father a dozen times. I dreamt about it as a child. At twelve, I became obsessed with shipwrecks.

"What color was the ocean that night? What about the next morning?" I asked my grandfather. "Did your pa tell you the color of the sky?" But he hadn't, though he'd seen it, hugging the paddle box for three days before being rescued, barely alive.

Even after my grandfather died, I kept asking. I asked my mother. Then I just asked myself. I began to draw the answers, then paint them. I wanted to find those women and children, my mother's drowned family, in the pigment on my canvas—not their vacant eyes, but the silent certitude of their descent. It seemed impossible to get those murky fathoms and the surface tension onto the same flat plane. After finishing art school, I'd washed dishes by day and painted that one blue acre at night.

Now the ocean was roiling on my canvas, waiting for me to contain it. The show was in four months. Postcards had been printed. I stayed up nights while Cash slept, but sure as the church bells in Mackville, he cried on the hour to be fed. I arrived at his crib angry, rushed, throbbing with milk. But the blue world fell away when he latched onto my breast. I often left slaked, fresh with ideas of what to do next. But it wasn't enough.

When Cash was ten weeks, the gallerist dropped by

unannounced wearing his signature orange bow tie and acid-washed jeans. The bright room was littered with large empty canvasses. I couldn't hide the strain. The *deconstruction* he'd once praised in my paintings, was now my life: grease-hardened dishes stacked on the floor, spilled turpentine, a used diaper on the couch.

While impressed by the large scale of my painting, he was disappointed by my progress. "What did I tell you?" he said, nodding to the infant in my arms.

"I'll finish," I said, hoping my smile was at least minimally seductive.

"I do like what you've got going here," he conceded, leaning against the stove. "The vibe is lighter, warmer, less frenzied. Clever, the way you're fracturing Diebenkorn." But I didn't care what he said. I'd been studying *Snow Storm* by Turner and *The Gulf Stream* by Homer—artists who'd painted the sea in 1854, the year the SS *Arctic* went down. The distress was still there, just millimeters below the surface.

Meanwhile, Grady came by almost daily asking to see Cash, never empty-handed, offering to babysit. He claimed to have the required skills and pointed out he'd only be alive for three more months, which didn't seem a good argument. He promised to wear gloves. I was tempted, but resistant, as uncomfortable with his tics and quirks as I was with his disease. At night, I argued with myself. If Grady were to mind Cash, he'd have to be close to him. Something might drip. Something might break or bleed. But the gallerist kept calling for updates. Each time Grady came by, I felt more distraught.

"You won't find free childcare anywhere else," he said one morning, standing with a bucket of Kentucky Fried Chicken at my front door. In the end, that clinched the deal. "Okay," I said. "We'll try." I had just enough savings for paint and rent.

Grady's babbling and Cash's warbling soothed me at first, wafting in from the fainting room, animating my brush strokes, but their unctuous call-and-response soon became maddening. Cash was crying now, full out, Grady trying to comfort him, using some goofy cartoon voice.

"He wants you," Grady called out. But I didn't want him to want me.

On my canvas, I saw the fading starlight over the Atlantic and the pale tendrils of dawn. I imagined the passengers, emigrants from Ireland, Norway, and Poland, the bodies of my mother's grandmother and her children decomposing below the surface. In addition to the SS *Arctic*, the *Powhattan*, *New Era*, RMS *Tayleur*, *City of Glasgow*, and *Guiding Star* all sank the same year, killing dozens of crew and hundreds of passengers, many of them poor, stuffed into cramped steerage compartments. The Atlantic was dense with human bodies no one could see.

I went to Cash's little room and leaned against the threshold, my painting shirt stained with milk.

"I need Cash out of earshot," I told Grady.

He looked up at me from the rocking chair.

"I'll take him for a walk," he said, with that puckish grin he had.

I almost hugged him.

Out on the landing, Grady's body seemed to be constantly repositioning itself ever so slightly in small lurches as if wings were emerging from his back. With Cash now snug in the stroller, I had second thoughts, this dying man at the helm. He'd float away if it weren't for his heavy-soled boots.

"Rock Hudson has AIDS," he said.

My head shot up from where I was kneeling to cinch Cash's safety belt. I'd watched *McMillan and Wife* with my mother when I was in junior high.

"He's gay?" I said. I had no TV and didn't read the news. Rock Hudson was my mother's heartthrob. She still had that photo of him in *Never Say Goodbye* on her fridge.

"Hollywood is in a panic," Grady said, scrunching up his face so his eyes became slits. He wiped his hands on his jeans. Two of his fly's metal buttons were open at the top. "They're deleting all his kissing scenes."

Cash was gurgling happily, his dark eyes bright with sunlight and fresh air.

I tried to ignore the purple lesions like paint on Grady's arms. He caught my stare.

"Cancer," he said, "is not contagious."

But I refused, at first, to let go of my grip.

"Please be careful, Grady. Come back by six."

I stood on the sidewalk and watched my neighbor's rubber-gloved hands guide the stroller down the street. He lifted his knees higher than most people, his rear end swiveling in his tight jeans, his shoulders moving from side to side like an old-fashioned washing machine. He almost looked confident. The stroller gave him balance.

Back in my apartment, months of exhaustion lay thick on my muscles and bones. I napped on the couch, then fretted far too long before finally getting back to work. The conversation I'd been having with myself—invisibility, viscosity, calamity at sea—slowly came back, muddled, like people talking under water. But I began to hear it.

Each painting in my *Arctic* series was distinct. The sky and whitecaps, the gradations of blue, the dark and light currents beneath the pigment. I'd used a range of brush strokes. My mother had sent me hog bristles from the farm; I'd splurged on fitch hair.

"Humanity defined by its absence," an art teacher had said in response to the early paintings. "Brilliant!" But it was the presence *in* the absence that I labored over with my rags and palette knives, my erasures and impasto—the wrecked memories of the lost.

Day after day, I painted and lost track of time, yet would always find myself standing on the sidewalk out front before six, my breasts aching with milk until I saw the tiny shapes turn the corner at the top of the hill and recognized Grady's skinny bowlegged swagger. From yards away, I could hear them, the tall one cackling, the small one cooing.

I always thanked Grady for his generosity. But later, under my artist's lamp, I'd pull Cash's diaper down and search his miniature genitals and anus, pushing at the skin like a monkey looking for lice. I'd examine his arms and neck. I never knew what it was I was looking for, sarcoma lesions or signs of abuse.

V

Every afternoon, as soon as the stroller rounded the corner, Grady took off the dishwashing gloves. At nearby Douglass Park, the sand had glass and dog shit in it. The plastic geodesic dome was scraped, weather-blistered, scarred with burns and teenage graffiti about gangs and fucking. "La Bamba" blasted from someone's boom box. Grady sat on the cement wall surrounding the miniature playground holding Cash in his arms, on the alert for errant baseballs and friendly, off-leash dogs. The baby's hands were elegant and perfect, the size of teaspoons— Cash himself seemed entranced by them every time they came into his view.

"Out of sight, out of mind," Grady said, laying Cash belly-down on the small blanket Llyn had packed, then lying down next to him. "Like you, little man. Gone. No Cash for Mom, no Mom for Cash." He worried about the boy's welfare. He was familiar with neglect.

"I lost my mom when my sister died," he said. "After that I lost everything."

Cash lifted his head and attempted to turn toward Grady as if he wanted to listen more closely to what Grady had to say.

"Father Rouquette had the biggest ears east of the Mississippi," Grady said, pulling his own ears out from his head to resemble his priest. Cash watched, then kicked and flailed his arms, suddenly rolling onto his back. His eyes searched frantically, then locked on Grady.

"We used to snicker in the pews," Grady said softly, then

switched to the scary wolf voice from "Little Red Riding Hood": "'The better to hear sin with,' Father would warn us." Grady stood up and lifted his arms as if he were Father Rouquette himself. "May Jesus Christ be praised!" he shouted, intoxicated by the thrill of confession in a public place. Two young mothers tightened hold on their little ones. A toddler decided not to go down the big kids' slide.

Grady knelt down just as he had in Belle Rose. "Bless me, Father, for I've been led astray," he said, playing himself. His best friend had taken him to the bayou's shoreline where, beneath a grove of cypress, Grady had learned the lust of tongues in the sulfuric air. He had been fifteen at the time. Now he was seventeen, sweating inside Rouquette's dark wood confessional.

"Tell me, son."

"I fuck men."

"I beg your pardon?"

That Sunday, Grady's mother had squeezed into a low-cut summer dress the color of ripe peaches, which made it difficult for the priest to focus on her mouth. *He's got the Devil's Disease, Father,* she had drawled, standing in the lobby after the service, *don't you, Grady?* She was more pious than prescient. She'd been referring to sodomy, not AIDS, which didn't exist.

Grady talked and Cash listened. The park looked brittle, like a video held on pause, in shifting white light.

Banished from Belle Rose by his mother and father, aunts, uncles, cousins, and congregation, Grady had headed west. He tried girls without luck, college without success, prostitution without remorse. Prone to involuntary twitching and deaf in one ear due to untreated syphilis, he was an easy victim for suburban teenagers who ambushed him on San Francisco sidewalks late at night. *Fucking faggot!* they yelled, punching and kicking him with such a vengeance they must have believed they could mold him into something else.

But there was something worse, he confessed to Cash, something he hadn't told Father Rouquette, or anyone else.

"Picture my mother," he said. "Tight white dress, arms and neck twinkling with trinkets. 'Don't you leave your sister's side,' she warned. 'I'll be back before midnight.'" Then she'd left the house to play One-Eyed Jack with the handsome highway patrolman who frequently stopped by in his Smokey Bear hat to compliment her on her roses.

"I was reading in the cellar," Grady said, then described how everything suddenly got quiet, outside and in, as if the earth had stopped spinning. How he'd heard his mother's tires on the gravel and run upstairs. The rest was a blank, but for Eva's blue skin in the morning and his mother's hysterical words: *You killed your sister.*

Cash sucked his pacifier as if he would die if he didn't.

"I know exactly how you feel, kid," Grady said, the memory ripping at his insides. And yet, with this confession, he felt buoyant, as if God Himself had dissolved the rancid knot in his throat. He put his index finger out in front of Cash's face and moved it slowly up and down and from side to side. Cash's eyes followed.

"Perfect!" Grady said, touching his finger to Cash's tiny

palm. Cash grabbed it. "That's it!" he exclaimed. "Fine motor control, little man. Soon enough, college. Then medical school to find a cure for this damn curse that's slaughtering us." Before long, no one was left in the park. The orange sun squashed down onto the roofs of the hillside houses. Tree shadows cooled the metal on the swings. The streets were quiet.

On the way home, Grady chattered about okra and alligators and the histrionics of parrots. He couldn't see Cash respond through the stroller's canopy so he pushed the brakes down with his boot and came around the front. Cash was beaming, his entire person so open and expectant it made Grady blush. The baby's mouth exploded with spoonfuls of liquid sound.

"You look absolutely mahvelous," Grady said, mimicking his parrot's rendition of Billy Crystal. Cash's face broke into his first true smile, tongue out and toothless. Grady whooped like a maniac. Earlier smiles had been lightning-quick and involuntary. This one was focused. This one was radiant.

VI

At the funeral, you remember things no one else remembers. But the priest doesn't ask you to speak.

Grady always told you with words what you did together in real life. He would make it like a movie, fast and in color. Like the pet store across the street from the park. Grady took you there since you were a baby in a stroller. A gazillion zoo sounds were like whirligigs in your head. Sometimes you tried to shake them out. The snakes and thorny iguanas said things only your inner ear could hear—that's what Grady told you later, when you were four. But the puppies whined and barked so loud you couldn't think. The kittens went mew, mew, mew in their small cages, all the tiny high notes. And the birds! Gigantic ones, tiny ones, pink ones, all the colors.

At first, you didn't even know their names. But now you do: canaries, cockatiels, finches squawking worse than fifth graders do at school assemblies with their silver flutes and golden trumpets.

Then one day, you were three and a half. You walked right up to the black-and-white toucan with its giant rainbow beak. Then—poof!—the pet store disappeared and the toucan flew inside your body like dreams do in sleep. You could feel the wings in your brain. Grady saw it! *Your heart built a nest!* he said. After that you could talk to flamingos and speckled owls and black-necked swans, all the birds at the San Francisco zoo. You could hear what they were thinking.

The pretty lady's big hair is flat from rain and she's standing by the headstone talking to all of you about Grady. Then a nurse talks. Then the doctor. Gracious, they say, which you don't understand. Miraculous, they say, which you do. Your mom says silly stuff like, I wouldn't be here without him.

No one asks you.

You would tell them things they never knew, especially your mom. Like what you did in Grady's apartment on Mondays when the pet store was closed.

Grady had an aquarium on the kitchen counter with neon

tetra that zipped around like little swimming flashlights, and silver-striped angelfish that moved slower than clouds and sometimes ate the tetra, and a California king snake in a large glass box that you and Grady fed mice to. Real live mice! He even had a parrot that said, *Hello Cash*, when you walked in. You asked your mom how a bird could know your name. But she was busy rinsing her brushes in the sink.

It was winter and you played tickling games on Grady's bed like Grady said he used to do with his sister. It rocked like a ship and you snuggled together like you hardly did anymore with your mom. Back then, she put up with you like the wobbly kitchen table she evened out with dimes. That's what Grady said.

At the funeral, the priest tells you to use the shovel to throw some dirt on Grady but you don't want to help him disappear. It's drizzling now and your mom kneels down even though she gets mud on her knees. So you kneel next to her in your suit and push a little dirt in with your hands like she does.

VII

March came and went. I didn't make my deadline. April passed, then May and June. Yellow roses bloomed in the back garden. It wasn't as if I hadn't tried. Night after night, I'd painted until dawn. In the mirror, I saw a Kentucky raccoon, onyx bands across my eyes. Knocks came regularly to my front door. If it was a loud rap, it was the landlord demanding rent. If it was a one-two punch, it was the gallerist. Soft, it was Grady. I begged East & West to go forward with the show using the eleven paintings I had, but the gallerist insisted on the agreed-upon thirteen. The last one I'd proposed—the largest canvas—was necessary, in his words, *to convincingly attract the smaller paintings into its orbit.* With the contract broken, we parted ways.

Grady, on the other hand, had been granted a stay. Mottled with sarcomas and wheezing, he bragged he could still guess the right answers on *Jeopardy!* before the contestants did. He took Cash to the pet store. He had color in his cheeks. I was the wreck, not him.

For the remainder of that hazy San Francisco summer and into the sun-drenched fall, I couldn't paint, my path forward suddenly choked with felled trees. I thought about getting my dishwashing job back at the restaurant, but could barely leave the house. I stayed in bed and let Cash play next to me on the floor, fitting little pots into big ones, banging silverware. Once he brought me a paintbrush and tried to comb my hair. He figured out how to stand up by holding onto my bed. From there, he often reached for me. He didn't know I was drowning, that if he grabbed onto me, he too would go down.

As the weeks went by, I began to derive pleasure from being adrift. I didn't answer the phone. Grady knocked, but I stopped going to the door. With no audience, I took pride in accomplishing the minimum: diaper changes, breastfeeding, canned peas mashed for Cash and warmed on the stove. Cash cried if I left him for even a minute. He called me *Mama* for the first time. Failure seeped from the drywall like mold and spread along the floor.

By September, my cupboards bare, I had no choice but to

go out for provisions. Grady was on the landing, shaking out his welcome mat. His cheekbones showed. He steadied himself against the railing. I was sure he was going to ask to take Cash for a walk, or recount some ghastly bit of news, but instead he asked me why I thought God had given him more time.

"You're just lucky, I guess." Above us, a thin strip of crystalline blue was visible between our landlord's roof and the one next door.

"I'll tell you one thing," I said. "He sure took away mine."

"Maybe this *is* your time," Grady said. "No pimped-up men in orange bow ties. No deadlines." He suggested I sit by the ocean, "since you seem to be obsessed with large bodies of water." I laughed. Back in Mackville, there'd been one small creek with a few catfish that dried up each summer, nothing more. So I drove to Ocean Beach with Cash, who scrabbled to the water's edge, chasing sandpipers that seemed to skate across the shore. He nursed and napped, then filled his bucket with wet sand and turned it over, again and again, until he'd built an entire city. I envied his industriousness. But the Pacific in person was nothing like the Atlantic I'd been imagining, the bleak cemetery sea I'd been investigating with my mind and brush for so many years. That deep, cold place, I realized, strapping Cash into his car seat, I could only find on my canvas. That night, after a hiatus of months, I began painting again. I let the ghostly swath of dawn at the top edge of #*12* filter over the entire canvas. I covered my failed blue acre with pale yellows and shades of white. Then I picked up a clean brush and started over. I drew the first blue line.

VIII

Grady called Llyn from the hospital that first time and asked her to bring Cash for a visit. Cash, one and a half, was walking and talking, dragging the wooden duck Grady had given him on a leash. His smile had teeth. Grady found it difficult to get through a day without him. Llyn, to her credit, had read the research and no longer required dishwashing gloves. Now it was the hospital itself she didn't trust: wards crowded with AIDS patients, life-threatening bacteria on every surface.

So Grady lay alone, his body numb between stiff sheets. Soon his eyes got too large on his shrunken face, and his legs and arms became bony and ethereal like the highest branches on trees. With no one to talk to, he imagined the nurse was the robin redbreast on the old cuckoo clock in the parlor back home in Louisiana. She would dash through the door every hour—pendulous breasts swaying—and wrap and unwrap the blood pressure belt around his arm, then zip back out, and he would be alone again.

A month went by. He felt as if a bag of plums was rotting in his chest. He could smell the sickening sweetness. With every difficult breath, he tried to retrieve another memory, but they crushed in his mind, like bluebird eggs in his little boy hands when he'd tried so hard to keep them whole.

Instead of memories, he had dreams with Cash in the leading role. Cash in Grady's father's arms whirling in a tornado. Cash in Grady's lap on a roller coaster ride. Cash at his sister's wake mixed up with cousins, the mayor, and Father Rouquette. Until, one day, his pneumonia got sucked out of him and he felt completely dry—a towel left out on the line on a long hot afternoon.

"My doctor gave me six months to live," he said to the receptionist on the way out. "But when I couldn't pay the bill, he gave me six months more!"

He'd heard the joke on TV.

The receptionist laughed, heartily, accidentally knocking a box of Kleenex to the floor. Grady leaned against her desk, barely able to stand.

"And six months more," he said, chuckling, "and then six months more."

They'd never met, but she extended her arm, showing off her ruby engagement ring, and invited him to her wedding the following year.

With his one good ear, Grady heard what he wasn't supposed to hear before the elevator closed.

"Maybe," the head nurse said behind him. "Maybe this one won't die."

IX

The knock at the door was like a faint heartbeat. I thought I was dreaming. Cash, almost two, clung to my leg. Through the viewing glass, Grady looked like a science project, creviced in odd places as though someone inside him was sucking him in.

When I unlatched the door, he was in mid-sentence. Something about a grandfather clock.

"You're alive!" I said. I meant to say *back*. His blue eyes were too luminous. His clothes were loose. He used a cane.

"I missed being home," he said, his voice barely audible, as though pounded and stretched over rocks. He tried to say more but coughed instead, doubling over. I put out my hand to steady him, ashamed I'd treated him more like a disease than a man.

"Up," said Cash raising his arms toward Grady, but Cash now weighed thirty pounds. Grady was too weak to lift him. He kneeled, nearly crumbling onto the landing. The two of them hugged for a long time.

"I can bring over some leftovers," I said. With my savings gone, I'd sold my car and my grandmother's wedding ring to pay the rent. Cash and I were once again surviving on ramen and baked beans. Before Grady could respond, Cash dragged him into his new bedroom, *the big-boy room*, the bedroom that had been mine.

I left them there and walked to the kitchen. Grady's funeral had been predicted multiple times, but today felt different. He really *was* dying. His annoying tittering, his liturgies of bad news, the dread, but also the relief I felt each time he knocked at the front door—everything I'd grown used to would be gone.

I sat down on the stool in front of my canvas. Cash's harmonica and the banging of his plastic drums filtered down the hall and into the room. While Grady was in the hospital, I'd worked feverishly at night while Cash slept. I'd finished #*12* and was now experimenting with a panorama of cerulean and

Phthalo blue, manganese and azurite, more chaotic and textured than anything I'd done before. It took up half my kitchen wall. I'd scraped away entire layers of paint, added more, smeared them off, scrubbed on more pigment, each layer heavier with oil than the one below it so the paint wouldn't crack or peel. I hadn't meant to suffocate the thing, but over the past few days, I'd quarreled so much with my canvas, I'd left it lifeless.

I should have relished this unanticipated moment, finally alone during my waking hours to study the problem and address it. And yet I had half a mind to join the silly orchestra in Cash's bedroom, to play "Yankee Doodle Dandy" on his kazoo. Minutes went by. I mixed the tints on my palette to replicate the lighter blue I'd just seen in Grady's failing eyes. I made a mark on my canvas, small, the color of cream, a reflection of light or, perhaps, a person. A little person, a child, floating, or drowning. Down the hall, the music grew louder. But I stayed with my painting, taken by this unexpected child, a speck in the cold ocean, so far from shore. I wanted him to survive. I tried one hue after another. None seemed right. I kept mixing, dabbing, trying various-sized brushes—inadvertently covering my original innocent mark—until I was exhausted and disheartened. Behind me, I heard Grady whistling and Cash's laughter.

I don't remember how I got there, but I found myself standing at the doorway to Cash's bedroom. Cash was clearly the conductor of their ensemble, ordering Grady to pick up the miniature green maracas, then attempting to blow into his harmonica, swaying his little body back and forth to the rhythm of their music together. I felt the exuberance of their love in the room and in the same instant its inevitable demise. I put out my hand to touch it. Or perhaps to protect it. They didn't see me. Their intimate world had its own space and time.

"Supper," I lied, wanting to break the spell that seemed to shut me out.

"No," Cash shouted, throwing his drumsticks. One hit the wall. The other hit my foot. Grady looked at me, abashed, his face ashen, as if it had all been his fault. I moved aside as he limped out.

"I'm sorry," I said to his back.

"No bye bye," Cash yelled, holding onto Grady's leg at the front door.

Grady extricated himself and gave a little bow before leaving.

A few weeks later, I woke to a siren cutting off in front of the house and Cash's howling. I ran down the hallway and swooped him up, then sat in the rocking chair and rocked him, something I hadn't done since he was a newborn.

We both heard the shouts of the paramedics, the gurney against the stairs, the siren fading in the distance. Cash wailed with a depth of sorrow it seemed no one his age could possibly have known. I offered him my breast, a pleasure we'd been unable to give up. But he refused. Nothing mollified him. His whole body shook with quick and noisy inhalations as though he couldn't catch his breath.

Can a heart that small be broken? I wondered.

Finally, he became quiet and peaceful and fell asleep on my

shoulder. I turned toward him, feeling his weight, inhaling his briny scent. I didn't move, not wanting to wake him, and we stayed like that until dawn, facing the wall that divided Cash's crib from Grady's bed on the other side.

X

Grady was disappointed not to see Cash as often as he once had, but the hospital had become a revolving door of admission, discharge, and readmission.

"You're a marvel," his suave doctor said, examining Grady's latest blood test results and shaking his head. "You really shouldn't be alive." He'd given up predicting expiration dates. But Grady, sitting sidesaddle, his thin legs covered with a sheet, felt the exam room caving in, not a quake that might stop the heart, but a slow darkening, a frightening feeling he couldn't push away.

It had been another dry winter.

That afternoon, Grady, watering the potted roses on his landing, heard a hollow, wailing sound like his mother had made at his sister's funeral, too hollow for this earth. It seemed to be coming from the shared garden behind the house. He found Llyn standing on the back porch wearing neon pink shades, so unlike her, Cash crying on the cement at her feet.

Llyn's hands flew to her mouth when she saw Grady. Had she hit the boy? One of her breasts was exposed, free of her bra and blouse.

Grady felt dizzy. He held tight to his cane, afraid he would fall or faint. Llyn closed her shirt and picked up Cash who kicked against her grip.

"Cash won't take my milk," she said as Cash wriggled out of her arms. "He won't breastfeed anymore."

Now *she* was crying.

A half-full sippy cup lay beneath a plastic patio chair. He wondered if she'd tried to force Cash to suck the last drips and drabs from her breast. She collapsed into the chair's curved shape, her arms hanging awkwardly by her side as if without Cash or a paintbrush she had no idea what to do with them.

"He's not a baby anymore," Grady said. His head hurt. The afternoon glare was harsh.

"You probably think I'm some sort of weirdo," she said.

"He's almost three, Llyn. Cash is a little man."

"But he still nurses at night. It calms him."

Grady suspected it was Llyn, not Cash, who felt calmed. He put his hand on her shoulder and she let it rest there.

"He's done with nursing," he said, a statement that got her weeping full throttle.

Cash was walking down the patio stairs, carefully putting two feet on each step, and into the small overgrown garden.

"I already miss him," she said. "It's like someone flicked the first domino and they're all falling."

Cash was in the garden, his back to them, studying something small as it moved slowly among the flowers. The neighbor's cat rubbed against him, back and forth as if searching for an entrance.

Grady felt it, too, each domino tumbling into the next one, clacking onto the table. He would never know Cash as a young boy: getting his first pet, learning to read.

Cash ripped a purple flower from its stem and held it up for them to see. Whatever Llyn's offense had been, it had been forgotten.

"That's a wild iris," Grady said, smiling down at him. But Cash was already onto something else.

"Birds!" he proclaimed, pointing to the trees. Late afternoons, the back garden tittered like an aviary.

"Those are sparrows," Grady told him.

Cash opened his fat little arms and waved them around, a miniature conductor.

"Grady," Llyn said. "How long will it be?"

"Before he goes away to college?" Grady asked.

"You," she said, surprising him by reaching from her chair to take his cool hand in her warm one.

At the hospital this last time, everything in Grady's body had seemed to be leaking into everything else. The entire apparatus that kept pee in the pee pocket, food in the food pocket, bowels in the bowel pocket; all this had broken down. "This," Grady had even laughed while speaking to the head nurse, "in a man who, how should I put it? I have always kept myself immaculate. I am very proud of that."

It would be soon.

Cash was singing now to the sparrows, mimicking their cheeps. Grady turned to Llyn slumped into the mold of her chair, but saw only himself reflected in her mirrored sunglasses. It seemed so long ago that he'd given up on the holy trinity he'd hoped for after Cash was born. But here it was.

XI

At three and a half, Cash was eligible for Head Start. I painted by day and waitressed evenings while Grady babysat. The familiar tinge of sadness I'd held at bay had taken up residence in my chest. Once again, I'd started over, calmly covering much of what I'd painted on the giant canvas. But this time, it wasn't enough. I'd begun to loathe the canvas's singularity of shape, its flatness and implied inertia. I needed simultaneous images all talking to one another: the sea my great-grandfather had witnessed on the day he was rescued, the sea my grandfather had described to me when I was a child, and the sea no one had seen. With a paring knife I cut the canvas into three panels, framed them myself, and connected them with hinges. A triptych.

For weeks I let my heart guide me, adding layer over layer, my approach and technique evolving as I went. I can't say exactly why or when but by spring, I was manic, painting dozens of miniatures on each panel, each one small enough to hold in the palm of a hand, until one morning I sat frazzled and spent in front of the three canvases and realized I'd been painting one for every woman and child left to drown that fateful September day in 1854, stranded without lifeboats by their fathers, husbands, and older brothers, abandoned against both policy and protocol by the healthiest male passengers and crew. I used a box cutter to whittle microcosmic fissures in the surface of each panel, exposing warm and cold currents fathoms below. I didn't know where in the landscape of contemporary painting my triptych belonged. I had no name for it.

Mika, who, like all my old art friends, rarely dropped by, visited me on a whim now that Cash was older. She couldn't hide her astonishment when she first saw the triptych leaning like three barn doors against the kitchen wall. The next day, she dragged her downtown gallerist to my apartment—the painting, by then, had become too heavy to move without the assistance of several large men. My slump was over. I signed the contract.

A few months later, Grady came to my opening reception, his skin a ghastly yellow. He limped even with his cane. Paul Simon's *Graceland* murmured its beat from large wooden speakers. The spiky-haired gallerist stood in the corner in plaid overalls with her arms crossed. Mika had brought a tablecloth and set up wine. A handful of people came. *#13* hadn't completely dried, which made it seem more alive, the two-room gallery fragrant with linseed oil.

Cash, almost four, sat cross-legged under the wine table with a stack of books, reading *One Fish Two Fish*.

"Read with me," he said when he saw Grady.

"In a minute," Grady said. "I'm looking at your mommy's paintings."

He took his time, standing at length in front of each one. I stood off to the side. Grady had never spoken to me much about my painting, nor had he ever seen the entire collection. After a while, he walked over to me.

"I see what you mean by *cemetery sea*," he said, quoting from my artist's statement in the program. Then he stopped in front of *SS Arctic #13*. "This one's not as cold as the others. It's not as closed." He somberly took the piece in. "It kind of brings all your paintings together."

I was reminded, then, of my old gallerist's stern pronouncement, unwelcome at the time.

"It's doing something big," Grady said. "I don't mean its size, which is *mahvelous*." He winked. "I mean what it holds. What do you think? It just goes and goes."

Was that what it was? Not presence in absence, or the unfathomable loss she'd felt as a girl on her grandfather's lap, but continuance?

Grady looked like he might collapse any second. I guided him to a wooden chair and sat next to him.

"It must not be easy," he said. "To paint everything you know."

I laughed. "Skeletons in the closet."

"Mercy is what I see."

He closed his eyes. He had almost no lashes and his lids were bluish pink.

"Remember last year when the Pope came to town?" he said, his eyes still closed. "He hugged a little girl with AIDS. He blessed her, Llyn. I thought *that* was mercy. Then the bastard laid his hands on guys like me and said, *Christ came into this world to save sinners.*"

"You're not a sinner," I said.

He smiled then as if he were thinking about something else entirely, then got up slowly, using his cane. He walked over to the triptych and touched the surface lightly.

"Don't touch the paintings," a gallery assistant said.

Grady turned to me. He had the blue of his eyes on his fingers. Then he did something strange. He anointed himself with the paint, touching his forehead and both arms.

Grady was a survivor, a man who'd lost pretty much everyone he knew. Like my shipwrecked great-grandfather, he was the last man standing. I saw him keenly in that moment, his astonishing fragility, but also his strength.

"How in the world did you get so much warmth into all that blue?" he asked.

"So you like it?"

"I love the little lifeboat."

"Where," Cash asked, coming over with his book. Grady pointed to a small light spot on the far upper right of the right panel. I knelt down for Cash to climb onto my shoulders, then stood up so he could see the aberration more clearly. Awash in one hundred and fifty square feet of blues, a small white mark with the thinnest line of crimson.

"Is that a little kid inside?" Cash asked.

"It could be," I said.

"Anything is possible," Grady said.

Cash looked doubtful. "Anything?"

———

At the end of that year, the landlord decided to move his elderly mother into our apartment and evicted Cash and me. We moved into a smaller, darker one-bedroom in the Excelsior District a short bus ride away. We visited Grady every weekend.

But two months later he wasn't there. We looked through the one small window, but the apartment was empty. We were sure he had died, but the landlord told us he had evicted Grady as well so he could tear down the dividing wall and combine the two apartments for his mother. We tried calling, but Grady's phone was disconnected. We waited together in front of the pet store. We tried the park. Cash said we should check the hospital, but when I called, I was told they were only permitted to give contact information to family. Of that we had no proof.

I got a part-time job as a receptionist and on my days off painted on the roof, the only place with sufficient light. Cash, a prolific reader, blazed through kindergarten. We often talked about Grady, reminding each other of details we wouldn't otherwise have remembered. We had a photo on the refrigerator of him holding Cash, at two, in his lap. As the months passed, he became almost mythical, as if he'd been a character in a book. Cash said Grady was like the older boys at the park who love to jump off the swing after pumping too hard, flying too high, but who always landed in the sand unhurt.

"Grady's a wizard," he said.

We both missed him.

A year later, I ran into his Cary Grant doctor on the street. I stopped the man. He didn't remember me but when I mentioned

Grady Delacroix, he said, "Oh, yes! My miracle kid." Grady was thirty-five the last time we saw him, but his doctor said *kid*.

"He's in hospice," the doctor said.

I was shocked he wasn't dead.

"Where's Hospice?" Cash asked me.

"It's not a place," I said. "It's a time."

Grady, it turned out, had been living with a roommate in a third-floor apartment near Dolores Park. The next day Cash and I took the bus to see him. I asked Cash to wait in the living room—not sure what I would find—but he insisted on coming with me.

Grady couldn't have weighed more than ninety pounds. He was lying on his side, looking out his bedroom window at a large avocado tree slick with light, his body completely still as if all his involuntary tics had finally gone to sleep. He was nearly deaf but he turned, his eyes diaphanous and calm, searching for us standing just inside his bedroom door. His partial dentures were on the nightstand; he couldn't hold them in, nor could he eat anything solid.

I couldn't move, watching him find us, but Cash went to his bedside and said hello and asked him where the parrot was and the snake and the fish and the mice. Grady smiled and took his hand. Cash bragged that he read five books a week, long ones with big words, and that when adding and subtracting dollars he knew where to put the decimal point.

Grady's eyes lost their focus but he didn't let go of Cash's hand. The hospice worker came in and said Grady needed to rest. He led us to the front door, but Cash refused to leave the apartment, so we played War with a deck of cards Cash found in the living room. I scolded him for sneaking all the kings and queens into his half of the deck.

"Grady taught me that," he said.

What else had he taught him, I wondered then, struck by how quickly our time had sped by and how much I'd never know.

A half hour later, Grady's bedroom door suddenly opened and we saw him run like an apparition, naked and smooth as a baby, right past us and to the front door, his skin glowing as if it were internally lit.

"We're still here," Cash said. But he wasn't looking for us. He was looking for his father, he said. He thought he'd heard the doorbell and that his dad was at the door, a man he hadn't seen in twenty-three years. It was as if Grady had risen from the dead from unrequited longing. He'd told me once his parents were long gone. When I'd mentioned this to Cash, he'd said, *Not gone from the earth, Mom, gone from Grady.*

When we came the next day, Grady could barely speak, gagging on a throat lesion. I wasn't sure if he knew us, or even knew we were there. His blue eyes seemed to be drowning, then floating, coming up for air.

XII

During his last days, there were things Grady tried hard to remember, but couldn't. Yet out of the morass, there was something he did remember, something he hadn't remembered. The way it really had been that terrible night in Belle Rose when he was twelve. There'd been no tires spitting on the gravel. His mother never came home that night, never called the family doctor at midnight, which is what she'd told his father. When young Grady had found Eva barely breathing, he'd run outside. He remembered exactly how the stars were, the Big Dipper and Jupiter blazing next to the moon. But his mother wasn't there. He didn't want to wake up the neighbors. He breathed into his sister's mouth. He tucked her blanket around her neck. She wasn't cold yet. She wasn't blue.

Where was his mother? He kept running outside, looking down the highway. Just before dawn, she turned into their circular drive. He was on the front lawn, his tennis shoes soaked with dew. What are you doing awake? she asked, her tone angry, walking toward him as she straightened her skirt. He knew now what she had done. In his final hours, in the dark of his mind, he wove in the threads.

XIII

You see the cemetery men put on their coats. They shovel wet dirt onto the coffin and add more until there is a mound the size of an upside-down bathtub. On top your mom places the yellow flowers she bought and you add the pink one you stole from someone's garden. Grady used to pick people's roses and azaleas and lilies—he called it a sidewalk sale—when he took you to the trolley that went to the main library. He let you pull the string when it was time to get off. When he read to you, he changed his voice for each character and there was nothing else in the world except Heidi on the mountain or Alice and the Queen of Hearts.

The rain has stopped. The crows are gone. But you know what they know. There are tasty lizards in the cemetery grass. Tonight, they'll be back.

The doctor holds his umbrella over the priest, so his bald head doesn't burn. Now that the clouds went on their way, the sun is too clean. His long robe is as white and loose as a pirate's sail. He's the only person who is dry, except Grady, who is sleeping in his body. You feel how totally gone he is now, like when someone's absent in class and their name is called and there's no one in their chair. Like what happened to him when his sister disappeared. A stick gets stuck in your chest like an ax in a tree. It's because of the stick, you want to tell Grady, that the feeling stays.

But the day is without him.

The doctor shakes your hand, which is how you know your heart has a temperature. He leaves first. His hair curls and he walks to his car without looking back, like a movie star. Then the priest hurries away, tripping on his muddy hem. Your mom puts her hand on your head and it sits there like a cap. Even now, it feels so good you don't even breathe. You don't move at all.

ACKNOWLEDGMENTS

It has been a long road from poetry to nonfiction to fiction, but here we are. Many have helped this particular book along the way, but early on, it was my soulmate Carmen Vazquez who told me in no uncertain terms that my voice mattered. It is her inimitable Nuyorican voice and those simple words that have propelled me through the fallow times, the troubling times, the doubts. Thank you, Carmen, for giving my flawed heart value.

An absolute hero years before I ever took a stab at writing fiction has been my literary agent, Felicia Eth, whose belief in my talents has been as staggering as her patience with my slow journey to completion of this collection. Thank you, Felicia, for your friendship and tenacity, through iceberg, storm, and calm, steering the way.

Cathy Colman, poet extraordinaire, my bestie since fifth grade, has always and generously conveyed her unlimited faith in me—heart, mind, and soul—and has been a reliably brilliant reader of my work as it hobbled along to the finish line. I couldn't have done it without her.

Many thanks to my numerous gifted teachers—my early poetry teachers: N. Scott Momaday, who, unlike others, embraced my untamed intensity, and Stan Rice, who taught me that poetry is the cinema of thought, *the physical treated with rapture come up to the level of idea*; and my fiction teachers at Bennington Writing Seminars and at summer writing workshops at Napa Valley Writers' Conference, Tin House, New Harmony, Juniper, and Bread Loaf: Lynne Sharon Schwartz, Amy Hempel, Askold Melnyczuk, Shannon Cain, Jim Shepard, Lan Samantha Chang, Charles D'Ambrosio, Stuart Dybek, Randall Kenan, Sarah Shun-lien Bynum, Yiyun Li, Anthony Doerr, and Joy Williams. But just as important have been my fiction workshop classmates, dozens of men and women over the years, whose close readings of these stories as they were developing gave them oxygen. I did not do this alone. Generous, honest souls poked and prodded the logs in the hearth, resulting in more warmth, truth, and fire.

Elena Felix is the self-proclaimed president of my fan club, of which there are no current official members. But that she, six years ago, even envisioned I might someday have a fan club, has been such a delight. Thank you, Elena, for making me feel like a queen when I had little to show for myself . . . and for keeping things jovial and light.

I am grateful to my local Bay Area writing groups, especially Jean Schiffman, Tanya Shaffer, and Turi Ryder, who grappled with my stories in their early stages, always with great enthusiasm and love, even when they were reading the same story, slightly revised, for the tenth time.

Thank you to my stalwart readers: Lauren Alwan, cotraveler into the world of fiction, always a few steps ahead of me, leading the way, and to Jennifer Hollmeyer, whose intriguing slant on my work sparked some of its most original moments. Thank you to Michelle Wildgen and Meg Storey at Tin House, who read my stories with relish and helped me see them as a collection for the first time.

I could not have written this book without contemplative places to go to in order to create without interruption, including fellowships at Ucross and Playa, but most importantly, year in and year out, a small spare room at Santa Sabina Retreat Center in San Rafael, where Directors Harriet Hope, for the first years, and then Margaret Diener, along with the entire Santa Sabina team—Elizabeth, Hector, Kathy, and Sara—always welcomed me as if I were family.

I am so grateful to my dearest oldest friends: John De Fries, Chris Leong, Bonnie Berg, Robin Koma Lee, Nelson Foster, Graciela Trevisan, Vaneida White, Amy Mueller, Anne Coffey Proctor, Tammie Knight, Richard Ingersoll, Mari Simonen, Colette Lafia, and Karen Sullivan; as well as newer friends: deTraci Regula and Corinne Quinajon, and so many others, who have applauded every small literary triumph, knowing how much each achievement has meant to me along the way. With special thanks to Erica Hunt, poet, mother, scholar, activist, who has had my back since grad school and has shown me how rich a literary life can be. Thank you to writer friends Lisa O'Kuhn and Karen Kao, whose insights on this collection were essential, even at the last minute.

Thank you to Sarah Gorham, Editor-in-Chief, and the whole Sarabande team: Kristen Renee Miller, Joanna Englert, Danika Isdahl, Emma Aprile, and Alban Fischer, whose spirited love for this collection was an honor and pleasure as they worked scrupulously to bring my debut collection into the world. Thank you to the judge for choosing *The Man with Eight Pairs of Legs* for the 2020 Mary McCarthy Prize in Short Fiction and to each editor and judge who has chosen some of these stories for publication. Thank you, Ladette Randolph, Editor-in-Chief at *Ploughshares*, for your kindness and for your unabated enthusiasm for the title story.

And finally, a big *mahalo* to my *ohana*: my unconventional Aunt Loreon, who inspired me to be an artist in the first place; my interested-in-everything parents, Caryl and Burnham, who would have wanted more than anything to hold this book in their hands; my delightful rebel sister Jaime, who always questions; my fellow Libra brother Bruce, whose insatiable creative spirit rivals my own; my generous, compassionate sons, Orlando and Jules, who were often the first to hear the good news—*Congrats, Mom!*—and grew up surrounded by bookshelves; Hatsumi, Deborah, Remi, Christina, Julia, Kamani and Kai; and my beloved husband Thomas, who, when he reads my work, always says *Wow!* or cries, and immediately imagines each story in Technicolor on the Big Screen—whose constancy gives my heart space and time.

"The Man with Eight Pairs of Legs" published in *Ploughshares Solos*, 2021.

"Thunder in Illinois" published in the *Briar Cliff Review*. Winner of the Briar Cliff Review Fiction Prize, 2014.

"City of Angels" published in the *Thomas Wolfe Review*. Winner of the 2019 Thomas Wolfe Fiction Prize, judged by Jill McCorkle.

"Nightlight" published in *Southern Indiana Review*. Winner of the 2013 Mary C. Mohr Editors' Award for Fiction, judged by Stuart Dybek.

"Tasmanians" published in *Arts & Letters*. Winner of the Arts & Letters 19th Annual Fiction Prize, 2018, judged by Amy Hassinger.

THOMAS SCHENKEL

LESLIE KIRK CAMPBELL's short fiction has appeared in *Ploughshares Solos* and won awards at *Arts & Letters*, *Southern Indiana Review*, the *Briar Cliff Review*, and the *Thomas Wolfe Review*. The author of *Journey into Motherhood* (Riverhead, 1997), Leslie is the mother of two grown sons and teaches at Ripe Fruit Writing, a creative writing program she founded, in San Francisco.

SARABANDE BOOKS is a nonprofit literary press located in Louisville, Kentucky. Founded in 1994 to champion poetry, short fiction, and essay, we are committed to creating lasting editions that honor exceptional writing. For more information, please visit sarabandebooks.org.